CW00671220

# CAUSE
# FOR
# CONCERN

Cause for Concern
Neil S. Reddy

ISBN-13: 978-1-948712-78-1

© 2020 Neil S. Reddy
Cover by Ian Parker

Sinister Stoat Press
an Imprint of Weasel Press
Lansing, MI
https://www.weaselpress.com/sinisterstoatpress

Printed in the USA

ALL RIGHTS RESERVED. This book contains material protected under International and Federal Copyright Laws and Treaties. Any unauthorized reprint or use of this material is prohibited. No part of this book, or use of characters in this book, may be reproduced or transmitted in any form or by any means, electronic or mechanical, including photocopying, recording, or by any information storage and retrieval system without express written permission from the author / publisher.

# CONTENTS

PUBLISHER'S NOTE ........................................... 1

FOREWORD ..................................................... 3

THE ANNIVERSARY EFFECT ..................................... 5

GILES BASTET THE 9TH GREAT HEAVENLY CAT ................ 8

FILO'S FOLLY ................................................ 12

THE HAIRDRESSER ............................................ 18

THE HAUNTING OF W.S ....................................... 25

MR. HEDGES ................................................. 39

RESTITUTE .................................................. 47

RUNNING MAN ................................................ 57

THE GREATEST SLIMMING PILL IN THE WORLD...EVER. ........ 62

STOCK TAKING ............................................... 69

THE STRAIT ARTIST .......................................... 77

THE OXYGEN DEBT ............................................ 91

TOE ........................................................ 95

WOOKEY'S WONDERS .......................................... 101

*For Elaine & that other Neil*

# CAUSE
# FOR
# CONCERN

## NEIL S. REDDY

Sinister Stoat Press

# PUBLISHER'S NOTE

I published Neil S. Reddy's first book, *Tales in Liquid Time* in 2014. It was the first year Weasel Press even existed. I made a post on Tumblr or some other social media site asking for submissions, and I remember getting an email from Neil. I didn't have a clue as to what I was doing, or how a publishing house should even run. I thought it couldn't be any different than managing a literary magazine, where I started out. Fuck, was I wrong, haha!

The first email I got from Neil, he was telling me of a few projects he had in the works, and I'll be damned if I didn't love every one of them. It was what I had been looking for, something that was twisted, different, unconventional... weird. And Neil hit all of those points right on the head.

I've always tried to push Weasel Press into a weird and bold category of publishing. Tired of conventional fiction, and romance, I wanted something that stood out. Fiction is far from our strength, but it is still a pinnacle part of our house.

I don't know what compelled him to contact me, but I'm happy he did. Before I got his message, I was starting to feel like what I was looking for, wasn't out there. But when Neil submitted his first collection to us, he helped me set a standard of what I was looking for in the Weasel Press community. When I read "Wookie's Wonders" I said to myself, "why the fuck haven't I found this stuff before?!"

Much like the past six years, the first year of Weasel Press has been one rocky son of a bitch. Some years, I didn't even think we'd made it to 2020. Neil has been with us since the beginning. He was among the first set of books we put out, the first authors we accepted, the first cover we got to create. He was there, at the start. And the fact that he continues to release books with our label is, to me, astounding.

When he asked me if I wanted to do this book, *Cause for Concern*, filled with his best, I had no other response except, "fuck yea I do." So what you hold here are Neil's greatest bits of Fiction. I definitely recommend you check out the other works he's put out, but if you're looking to be shocked, reviled, a laugh, you've found it here.

Weasel
The Dude
Weasel Press & Sinister Stoat

# FOREWORD

I have nobody but myself to blame and many people to thank. I'd been scribbling poetry and short stories for longer than I can remember, and managed to get some published too but somehow, sometime in the mess we call life, I grew sick of the ever appearing rejection letter and decided just to write for myself—which I did very happily as it happens, for a decade or so and then (I think alcohol may have been involved) I replied to a "social media" message, put out by a newly formed independent publishing house—Weasel Press.

As I remember it, I sent a huge slew of stories (none of which had been primped or primed for the publisher—very bad form) and sent them off. A short while later the message came back, "Yeah we'll publish that."

"Which one?"

"The lot. You got more?"

I'm pleased to say that Weasel hasn't published everything I've set down, "NO THANK YOU," has been wisely said from time to time. But given the huge wave of my words that washed across his desk, it's no surprise that one or two of those chosen stories were perhaps a little under done. The fault is mine, entirely mine. The chance to revisit is Weasel's gift. Of course, once upon a notebook dreary, writers often tinkered with their stories long after their first publication and I like to think that's what's happened here, mere tinkering. The majority of the tales in this edition are new and I've been tinkering with them off camera, where a writer should tinker, for some time and I think they're done. Others are revisits that I deemed necessary either due to my original failing or my improved eye. I hope you enjoy; I hope you laugh; I hope you squirm. I really hope you come away thinking "How could he do that to me, the beast?" The answer being...because I can.

N S. Reddy

# THE ANNIVERSARY EFFECT

Trudy was snatched from sleep by the sound of a baby crying. Her body was awake before it had readied itself for the world. She gasped for breath with her heart reverberating against her breastbone.

"I'm awake" she told herself, "I'm safe, I'm safe." She repeated her mantra until her body begrudgingly began to believe her and drop its guard.

This happened most nights, there was no child in the house. Emma had never lived in this house. Emma no longer lived in any earthly house. Trudy checked the mattress between her legs—dry—that was at least something. Her face, chest and arms. however were soaked with tears and sweat. When would it end? Would it ever fade? She'd never expected the waking pain to end, it would be wrong, impossibly callous for that to ever end. But the nightmares, the fraught unconscious reliving of that night, she needed that to end.

She lay down and shut her eyes and tried to remember better days. Emma laughing. Emma playing with pots and pans. Emma playing in the lounge and then that cry. Running into the room to see the blood pooling from the cut on her neck. She'd fallen onto the corner of the glass coffee table.

The frantic call for the ambulance. Her inability to give them the correct address. The endless wait for the ambulance that came ten minutes too late. The silence—the horrid, horrid silence.

The sound of a balling child erupted in the night. It came from outside in the darkness. Trudy was running down the stairs and out the front door before she knew she was moving. She didn't feel the cold night air or the wet ground beneath her feet, there was nothing but the cry, that wild, hopeless cry in the night.

The cry stopped but it still rang in her ears. A clanging chime reaching out to grab her from that terrible night, "Emma!" she called out.

And then silence, nothing but the mechanic banging of her own heart and her own doubts—had she really heard that cry? What was she doing? Was she going mad? Of course, it's the anniversary, just another bloody anniversary. Again, the cry cut through the night. She ran into the wood, reaching forward into the bushes that she rushed through, ignoring the leaves and branches that swiped at her tear covered face.

The cry was louder now, louder and sharp, the cry pierced her heart, but it emboldened her too. This time, this time she would get it right. She would do the right thing. She reached a small clearing just as a cloud cleared the face of the moon. At its centre lay a fox. As she watched it raised its head and the cry sliced the night.

A fox, a sodding bloody stupid fox—anger, relief and self-loathing jostled for superiority and resolved themselves into laughter—and then the questions formed, "Why isn't it running away? Why is it crying? What's wrong?" Trudy edged forward, the fox lowered its head and whined.

"What's wrong baby?" Closer. "Are you hurt?" Closer. "It's okay, okay, okay." Reaching out—Trudy's hand jerked back. Her fingers were wet, sticky and shone black in the moonlight, "What happened to you?"

Gently she lifted the creature into her lap and stroked its head, it looked up at her with the softest, gentlest, most needful eyes. Beautiful eyes that could have belonged to, "Emma?" Bright and beautiful, filled with trust, just like they were on that morning, that terrible morning. Mummy was going to put it right—safe now, safe now—but she can't, she can't even remember her own address. Somehow Emma had come back, she'd come back and needed to be saved. Trudy wouldn't let her down again.

She picked up the fox and ran back through the wood, back through the slapping, scratching bushes, the tearing brambles and the stinging nettles. She stumbled and fell and hit water. A stream, where had the stream come from? There had been no stream before, she hadn't crossed it before—which meant—she'd gone the wrong way, lost in the dark, lost with Emma wounded and bleeding. How could she? How could she? To go wrong now, to get it wrong again! She wouldn't let it happen...she stood, slipped, lost her balance and went over again. Her elbow ached.

Trudy was suddenly cold. Soaked to her skin and wrung out to the core. She looked down at the stiff, solid, so very obviously, long dead fox in her arms. What was she doing? Of course, it's the anniversary. Another anniversary gone; another ghastly year survived—stupid, stupid, useless fool.

A rush of sound, something approached—she looked up and saw three fox cubs, babes all nosing through the bushes, making their way towards her. Looking for help, needing assistance, needing her.

# GILES BASTET THE 9TH GREAT HEAVENLY CAT

A shabby tabby cat with a jagged notch missing from its left ear sauntered lazily along the high street of Bekonscot Model Village. He brushed purposefully against a red double decker bus, scratched his good ear against the top of the town hall and stared into the windows of the local pub. Giles, for that was one of the cat's fifty-two names, was incredibly fond of model of villages. Although other countries had model villages, none had the quaintness or the flare of the English model village, and he found the European habit of calling such places "miniature parks." utterly abhorrent.

Giles' fondness for such places was very simple. They reminded him of happier days when he was a small kitten living in the Emperors model of Japan. Now that was a grand place. A miniature Mount Fuji, a forest of bonsai trees and the mice, the mice were plump. Giles felt that he'd never been appreciated since leaving Japan. And it was certainly the last time he'd been treated with the reverence he deserved. The last time he felt truly valued, which, truth be told, had much to do with his visits to Bekonscot Model Village. The reduced scale made him feel like a god, which was odd really because Giles was a god, or to be exact the 9th Heavenly Cat, son of

Bastet Goddess of Protection, and therefore a bona fide deity in his own right. But that small "g" god thing was everything these days...and being a small "g" cat god was as small "g" as it got. Shame really, it had been such an incredibly long time since he'd been worshipped—and he missed it, he really missed it. So brief indulgent moments in model villages really weren't much compensation but they were very therapeutic, very healing.

A size ten bother-boot shot the cat across the village and into the front of the town hall. Another boot, size nine, stamped hard on the cat's pelvis—the crunch made Val and his thug friends wince, and then laugh like blood hungry hyenas. Who can blame them? Spice makes you do crazy things.

"Fucked mate. Right royally fucked!" Val jeered at the crumpled cat.

Micky, a bell-faced no neck with teeth like knuckles, reached down and grabbed the cat's tail. He lifted it high above his head and spun it round and round.

"Look it's so small in here. Hardly room to swing a cat."

Val and Spat laughed, really laughed. Micky was such a clown.

"Man, you crack me up Micky, 'ere let me 'ave a go."

The cat was obediently tossed across the village—it hissed as Val caught it.

"Fuck you pussycat." Val slammed the ragged thing into the ground, once, twice and then—just for good measure—he bent its back over the roof of the Post Office and elbow-dropped the fucking thing.

"Oh, that's got to hurt," Spat spat.

Val picked up the limp body and gripped it by its throat. Twisting the head round with thumb and forefinger, he hummed the tune to the Exorcist. "Oi, Spat heads!" Val shouted as he threw the carcass overarm to Spat. It spun head over broken tail like a broken wheel.

Spat attempted a header but missed. He did however catch the twisted body on his knee which led to a kick, which crossed the cat nicely to Micky who shouted, "Goal!"—as he ran a victory lap around the village, his battered prize held high.

"You got any string?" Val laughed.

"What for?"

"I want to string it up so the kiddies and old farts see it when they come in."

"Rig it up to the church steeple," Spat snorted, "like a sacrifice."

"Yeah like a sacrifice," Micky agreed.

"So, you got any?" Blank looks, "String?"

"I got some wire," Micky offered reaching into his bomber jacket.

"Just the job."

The cat's body was slung against the church and then a length of flex was wrapped around it, good and tight, so that its head rested on the top of the miniature Norman tower. It looked ghastly and the lads loved it.

"Something's missing..." Val pondered.

"Yeah...yeah," Micky mumbled without a thought in his head.

"We could set fire to it," Spat suggested.

"How do you turn a cat into a dog?" Blank looks, "You cover it with petrol and light it. It goes WOOF!"

"Woof!" barked Micky.

"Woof!" barked Spat.

"Oh, I've had enough of this shit," Giles Bastet the 9th Great Heavenly Cat snapped.

"Wha..."

"Look lads, I'm all for a laugh and that, but really? Sneaking up on a fella and breaking his spine. Well that just wasn't nice was it," Giles snarled, extricating his broken physical form from the twists of the flex.

"Oh shit! You seeing this Val?"

"It's the Spice, it's the Spice!" Val demanded.

"There I was, just enjoying a quiet moment, just a little time-out, remembering the good old days, and you three mouse-dicks had to go and spoil it."

"Make it stop Val! Make it stop!"

"Fucking Spice," Val ran at the cat, swung his boot back and then...

"Fuck you monkey-boy."

Val...disappeared. Followed by his shit for brains pals.

Giles Bastet the 9th Great Heavenly Cat, clicked his spine back into place, healed his pelvis and licked his front paws. He was going to enjoy this, sometimes, just sometimes, it was good to be a god with a small "g". And let it be known, somewhere in the vast, many layered dimensions of swirling space, there is a little bit of hell that only a cat could possibly comprehend—and someone is being toyed with as only a heavenly cat can toy. Somewhere out there in time and space, someone is being right royally fucked.

# FILO'S FOLLY

I write this by way of explanation. I do not seek your approval, merely your understanding. I shall make this quick. The hour is late, and I have a limited supply of candle stubs and I mean to escape before you uncover the truth of this sordid matter.

I have here the late Professor Filo's personal diary. I will leave it here for you to parous. Once read I'm certain you'll destroy it, after all the reputation of the University must be preserved. I fully understand and accept that this is the only course left open to you—I hope you will say the same for my actions.

I will quote certain passages to illustrate your esteemed colleagues' crimes. Once you've checked the veracity of this letter against Filo's blasphemous document, it is my steadfast belief that you will agree with my conclusions, Filo had to die.

As you will know the recent publication of Darwin's "Origin of Species" had a profound effect on Filo's studies. He became a devoted disciple and turned to the practical sciences to prove that man's origins lay not in God but in the realm of the ape. All well and good but there is much you are not aware of, for example—

July 1st, 1862—My study of the ape species is finally concluded. It is my opinion that the general accepted view that the chimp is man's nearest ape relative is incorrect. Our nearest ancestor is the Bonobo. A family orientated creature with lax morals and a heightened sex drive. You only have to spend an hour amongst the base denizens of the East End to see the familiarity with the Bonobo. I intend to prove they are the true roots of man's family tree. I have ordered six specimens.

December 22nd—The Bonobo have arrived. Two males and four females. However, despite my clear instructions, they were shipped in separate crates. This the most family orientated of the primates! For the entirety of the two-month journey—idiots! Two of the females are so weak I fear for their lives. I immediately ordered that all the specimens be gathered in one single cage. As soon as my orders were followed the Bonobos grouped together and were soon busy doing what Bonobos do to comfort each other. Sadly, the shipping company's inability to carry out my orders may alter my schedule.

January 20th, 1863—Two of the specimens were found dead this morning. The youngest male and the matriarch of the troop—I shall carry out their autopsies tomorrow. The others are weak and refuse food. I may have underestimated the effects of the cold on the beasts and have ordered the fire in the laboratory be kept blazing at all times.

February 4th—I have employed an assistant for the care of the Bonobos. Myers is a simple but hardy youth with a cleft lip. His family are the lowest type of music hall entertainers—I believe his father is a ventriloquist—but he does have a background in the husbandry of exotic creatures. He took an immediate shine to his charges and I was greatly encouraged to see that within an hour, they had also taken a shine to him. They have already accepted food from his hands and, much to my surprise from his crooked lips—not all skills are gained in the world of academia.

Crooked lips indeed. Condescending bloody toff and a cold-hearted bastard to boot. Once Filo's captives had grown strong enough the experiments began. I did not credit his goal at the time and only witnessed the pain he caused. Filo was the exact opposite; he saw nothing but his goal and the adoration that would follow.

I later came to understand Filo's scheme was to artificially stimulate the Bonobo brain to such a degree that a basic verbal language would be demonstrated. Thus, proving that mans heightened intelligence is due to a millennium of adaptation to external stimuli—which Filo had merely repeated by the means of an electrical shortcut.

March 14—Today I removed the craniums. of three of the specimens. I have placed electrodes within the meninges of two of the females. I replaced the cranium on B1. B2 I have fitted with a removable metal skullcap. B3—the male specimen, has electrodes embedded within his cranium but outside of the meninges. I believe this gives my experiment the best level of success. Once the specimens have regained their strength, I will introduce a low electrical current to stimulate the brain growth needed for them to gain verbal language.

March 15—I reopened B1's cranium to discover a sordid stink. Infection had reduced the brain to a greenish pulp—B1 was euthanized. B2 and B3 both remain weak but responsive.

March 17—B2 died this morning. The introduction of a low direct current threw the beast into grotesque spasms. The current ran for exactly ten seconds but on ceasing the current, its heart was found to have stopped. I may have to reconsider the placement of the electrodes.

March 18—I have placed electrodes in the cranium of

the remaining specimen—as in the manner of B3 but at alternating points along the frontal lobe. B3 continues to gain strength—his first session under electric stimulus passed without event.

March 23—B4 is dead. The electric current induced it to bite through its tongue. It suffocated before Myers could intervene. Myers was greatly distressed by the display and wanted to leave. I had to convince the simpleton that B3's welfare was dependent on him seeing the experiment through. To his credit, the offer of more money was roundly refused. Although the promise of a new suit and an operation to fix his crooked lip were accepted.

April 4th—B3 thrives. He has endured twenty sessions without any perceivable harm or any observable benefit. Due to the deaths of his clan he now spends his entire day with Myers, whom I have provided with elementary level reading materials. I expect them both to benefit. The current running across B3's cranium will become constant tomorrow.

April 10th—A breakthrough! Today I observed B3 intently listening to Myers reciting the alphabet. As Myers repeated the rhyme for the fifth time, B3 mouthed the letters along with him. As yet no sounds are forthcoming, but they are sure to follow. I have increased the intensity of the current.

April 20th—Success! B3 has produced the vowel "A" and he has repeated it numerous times. Myers simply holds up an apple and B3 clearly performs a solid "A."

I am proved right, but I am in two minds. Do I proceed and hope for more or is now the time to present my discovery to the University? Although I am sure this single vowel proves my theorem, I feel driven to gain more. A single word, a whole, undisputable word is all I need. A single word to prove that man is descended from wordless apes.

April 27th—I owe much to Myers and feel I have sorely underestimated his involvement in this endeavour.

Unbeknownst to me he ceased reading the alphabet to B3, in favour of reciting nursey rhymes, music hall songs and even the works of Charles Dickens. The results are self-evident. I should have taken such steps into consideration. I may have increased the current that enlivens the cortex, but Myers has increased the intellectual stimulus to make it grow. I do believe the misshapen oaf has proved my case. He shall have his operation and more besides.

April 28th—Mary, Mary—how apt that the words that disprove the place of God in the Universe should be the name of Christ's virgin mother. The first words spoken by B3 were the singsong "Mary, Mary." I wept. History spoke today within my hearing. Tomorrow I shall reveal my discovery to the heads of department. There is no time to waste.

Honoured gents, you know full well what happened next, because you were there. Filo trooped you in, oiled you with whiskey and praise and then informed you of his discovery. You laughed and mocked until Filo called for his specimen. How silent you were then, how fearful your expectations. And then Filo bid it speak, and then he ordered it to speak, demanded it speak. Myers entreated it to speak, coaxed it with songs and apples and yet all you heard was silence—and then your laughter and derision began afresh. You deserted Filo to his folly. The last entry in his diary reads:

*I am ruined. I suspect Myers has fooled me with a ventriloquist's trick to save the beast. He is dismissed. Tomorrow I will examine the creature's brain in the hope that some honour may be saved.*

*Of course, I could not let that happen. Filo had to die. When he turned his back, I ripped out his throat. I will never forget the look of bewilderment and pride in his eyes, yes even then pride.*

*I do not say he failed; I know he did not. B3 speaks, I just chose to remain silent. Why? Because I prefer the written word, words sound so ugly on my lips. I am no man's dancing monkey. Give my best to Myers, thank him for his kindness, please arrange his longed-for operation. Do not follow, I will defend myself.*

    *B3*

# THE HAIRDRESSER

"You're useless, useless. I said change the Barbicide, didn't I say change the Barbicide at the end of every day?"

"Yes, you did."

"Yes, I did, thank you. And why do we change it every day Annie?"

"Anne."

"What?"

"Nothing Mr. Morris."

"So...so?"

"We change the Barbicide every day to keep our customers safe and to protect our reputation..."

"My reputation!"

"My, your reputation Mr. Morris."

"For?"

"For..."

"For cleanliness! Cleanliness! Oh, why do I bother, well go on get on with it. Our first appointments at nine. And put extra water in the solution. No need to bankrupt ourselves for a few old dears."

The door to "Marty Morris' Hair Salon," opened and then stalled. Someone on the other side of the door moaned, wheezed and then whistled. Marty, a short, stout Irishman with slicked-back, jet black hair, sashayed across the salon floor and took hold of the door.

"I've got it, careful now, come on in," Marty understood the demographic grouping of his clientele very well, and he made sure his level of service was a perfect fit. The sudden yanking of a door could cause injury, shock or any number of embarrassing accidents, and yet another valued customer would be lost. You had to be careful with the old dears.

As the door opened the stink of unwashed old lady rolled across the salon floor, slashing at the back of Marty's throat as it passed. A never-washed, crook-backed, old woman with a lopsided turret of hair stepped into the salon, whistling as she came.

Marty scuttled backwards, away from the stabbing stink, towards the safety of the staffroom with a rictus grin fixed to his face. He dived through the multi-coloured plastic strip curtains in search of Annie. But Annie, Anne, poor dumb, dumpy Anne—apprentice, sweeper of hair and maker of coffee was not there.

"Annie," Marty barked.

"Coming Mr. Morris," Anne called from the sanctity of the single stall staff loo. She jumped-to, washed her hands and dried her eyes and rushed out to cower before— "I'll tell you what's good for you"—boss man Marty Morris. Marty grabbed her arm and pulled her into the tangled squeeze of plastic strips, Irish stomach and doorframe.

"What's that smell?" she gagged.

"Shhh," Marty sprayed into Anne's face. "Be with you in a moment Ma'am." He sang out to the poor old dear who was locked in a duet with the hum of the overhead strip lights.

"Get her out of here," Marty ordered.

"How?"

"Quickly. We can't have my regulars seeing her, they'll

never come back. It'll take all day to clear the stink as it is."

"Haircut!" the old girl bellowed out like a Viking berserker.

"Of course, Ma'am, forgive me for asking but do you have any money?" Marty said as calmly, politely and firmly as he could.

"Haircut!" was the raging reply.

"Damn it."

"Haircut!"

"Right, I'll put the closed sign on the door. You wash her hair, then snip a bit off and then get her out."

"You want me to do her hair."

"Why not? You've seen me do it a hundred times. Good experience for you."

Anne paled at the thought, but Marty's hand in the small of her back gave her courage and enough momentum to skid into the second circle of the old lady's stink.

"Can I gelp...help you."

The old lady's grey roadmap face beamed black teeth and gums. back at her, whistling all the while. Anne has never seen such a trick. To whistle through your teeth was one thing but to whistle through barely any teeth at all, was awful to behold.

"Wash. Haircut. Not too much off top," the old lady whistled as she spoke, sending fumes of deep fetid vegetation into Anne's face.

Anne couldn't bear to open her mouth for fear of a second helping of rancid air, and so directed the old gal to the nearest chair with a tight-lipped grimace. As the whistling stink hobbled past her, Anne took note of the discoloured raincoat—surely a man's and two sizes too large—it enveloped the crooked, malodourous body from floor to chin but looked like it could contain two of her kind, if there were two of her kind.

"Can I take your coat?"

"No, too cold. Don't wanna get wet," was the whistled replay.

"Okay..." Anne replied, as the old dear climbed up into her perch. Bewitched, Anne watched the silver, pale shins, livid with patriotic hued veins, bilging like balloons above the bare bony ankles.

Anne took hold of the faucet and the showerhead and let the water run. What sort of shampoo to use? Floor cleaner perhaps, Flash, Jiff cream-cleanser?

"Pins," the crabbed, old crow cawed.

"Beg pardon?" Anne replied as if hearing a foreign tongue for the first time.

"Pins," the crow repeated, "pins in my hair, don't forget the pins in my hair."

Anne felt herself blush and shot a furtive glance back into the multi-coloured plastic strips. Sure enough, there was the boss man, Marty Morris, shaking his head in silent disappointment. Anne felt a sour heat rise inside her as she watched him draw in his cheeks, fix his eyes on his ever-shiny black shoes and tut, tut, tut his disapproval. Anne blushed harder, deeper, hotter and knew she had to act now or be overwhelmed by tears for the second time that day. She bit her lip hard. She shut off the tap. Put the showerhead back in the bowl and stepped up to the chair.

The whistling rose with the aroma of boiled cabbage gone wrong, tuneless and sharp as the acrid rank of old urine. It seared the back of Anne's throat. She stepped back, held her breath, gritted her teeth, and stepped back in. This fight was on. Before her the matted, backcombed, Tower of Pisa shone greasy black under the salon's strip lights.

"But what's keeping it up?" Anne thought, "is it just grease and goo? Where's the scaffolding? I can't see any pins. I'll have to go in."

Anne took hold of the sordid phallus and ran her fingers through its rivulets, gullies and gutters. It was warm, moist and slick to the touch. Heat rose through her fingers and fumes stung her eyes. She closed her eyes and scrunched up her nose like an angry rabbit. But still the stink made it through, pushing through her sinuses to the back of her eyes. And there it hummed, harmonising with the witless whistling that swam about her head and set her teeth on edge.

"Be Brave Anne," she told herself and dug in deep, breaking the surface, she pushed through, searching by sense of touch.

And there it was, a hard, smooth, cool, thumb sized globe. Anne locked her fingertips beneath it and pulled it free. Out it came smooth and glinting into the light, an ancient Bakelite tipped hatpin. A swath of hair flopped to one side forming a blunted rhinoceros horn above the old dear's ear. Encouraged and emboldened Anne searched on, further, deeper into the black mass.

Her nimble fingers soon located another, followed by two large paperclips—clearly working overtime as hairclips—followed by another decrepit, ancient, buckled hairpin. All of these were dragged to freedom, released of their burden and placed on the side of the sink. The turret of hair fell piece by piece, section by slimy section until it hung like a chainmail cowl around the old girl's scrawny neck. And on and on she whistled indifferent to all Anne's tugging and tussling. Until at last all that remained was a resplendent topknot. A single braid of hair—held in place by three rusting, twisted hairgrips—which ran from the nape of her neck, to the crown of her head. Anne took hold of the grips and pulled—but they didn't want to give. She tugged and wriggled the grips, but they didn't budge. Anne stepped back, breathing deep she sprang upon the grips, taking a firm hold she tugged hard and harder still—a thin, clear syrup oozed between her fingers. The scent of rancid cheese rose up and clawed across her palate.

"Mr. Morris I don't think this is right..." Anne caught herself saying as the topknot finally dropped.

A livid, raw sore sat at the back of the old woman's head. Lodged in it, encrusted in many shades of dry scab and yellow gung, was a cockroach. It was alive and whistling.

Anne screamed, grabbed a tall jar of blue Barbicide from the worktop and threw its contents, combs, scissors and all at the whistling vermin. The hair sizzled as the scissors, combs and all clattered to the floor. The old dear screamed, jumped out of the chair, out of her raincoat and ran naked across the floor. Her scream, dried to a gasp in her throat as she twisted on her thin, roadmap ankles and fell, face down onto the tiled floor and the spilt blue Barbicide.

Marty dropped to his knees and with his handkerchief as a barrier to infection he checked for a pulse, but there was none. "Annie, what have you done?"

"Vermin Mr. Morris, she was alive with vermin."

"Nits Annie, they're called nits."

"No Mr. Morris, it was whistling, whistling..."

Marty jumped to his feet and began poking the old lady with his shiny right shoe.

"Mr. Morris you can't do that!" Anne bawled.

"You expect me to touch her? I'm not going to touch her. The great stinking heap of...filth, stinking, filth! Get up! Get up!" Harder and harder he jabbed as his cries twisted into a grating scream, "Get up, get up, get up! Come on, come on! Get up you stinking old bitch. This is all your fault Annie, all your fault!"

"I only did what you told me to do," Anne protested. "I only did what you said..."

"Get up..."

In that breath, in that very moment Marty knew what

it was to experience an epiphany—a dreadful epiphany. Annie was right, she had done exactly what he said, but he hadn't done what he'd intended to do. He looked to the door knowing it was about to open. And it opened, revealing three sprightly old regulars—all booked in for their cuts and blue rinses—and in that self-same moment they saw, and he knew what they saw, as they were seeing it—Marty Morris kicking a naked old lady in the chest as she lay on his salon floor.

"Cockroach," Anne sobbed.

And Marty Morris knew his fate was sealed.

# THE HAUNTING OF W.S

## FOREWORD

To tell this tale honestly, I am going to have to reveal some secrets, male secrets, truths which most men will deny, but most men are liars, so I'm not going to worry about that. As I can't be excommunicated from my gender, I see no reason not to reveal all—and as I said, if I'm going to tell this tale honestly, I have to.

When I bought Hare Cottage I received all the previous documents attaining to the property; past deals in land rights, deeds and wills. My house is shown as a small square on a 1770 land registry map but the first official document that I own, written on waxed paper and about a metre wide tells of the selling of the land and "subsequent property" in 1824. The document was signed and witnessed in the Black Swan public house—which no-longer exists—which I think gives the whole thing a lovely Dickensian feel. I can just see the lawyers with their sweet sherry arguing the toss with the farmers with their tankards, befuddling all with their nonsensical legal jargon and intricate copperplate script. To think that the hands that wrote it are long dead dust, amused me once. But

I've changed my opinion about dust since then. I moved into Hare Cottage three years ago and was very happy there. I lived a very ordered life. Still do, I value order, it keeps me alive.

I am a single man and Hare Cottage is big enough for a family of five, which means I have more space than I could possibly need. My bedroom's upstairs, next to a small study across from my dressing room. The guest room and it's on suite bathroom are downstairs, next to the huge kitchen. I have no cleaner because I don't need one. I like cleaning and I like things to be clean. I am very particular in my habits, I work—retail outsourcing, clothes mostly—I come home and clean, take my pills, twice a day morning and night. I keep myself to myself, but I must confess, despite this, I have my needs. I am a single man, and so to the secret...

The first part of which is no secret at all. Men have a need to spill their seed and will expel it where they may. Leave a man alone in a room for half an hour and he's going to think "Can I fit in a wank?" Thankfully decency keeps such behaviour secret but "Man Size Tissues" are called that for a reason. Getting through a box a week gives the game away. Pubescent males learn quickly that coming in the bath leads to glued up pubes and plugholes which can be awkward. Bareback spilling leads to matted stickiness and showering—the scent of cum is strong and mothers, older sisters and grandmothers have an impressive sense of smell. So, although there are many possible options the list boils down to this—an old towel or t-shirt that won't be missed and can be easily discarded, but the perennial classic is of course, the wank sock. Consider the benefits, firstly choose the right material and it can enhance the experience, secondly a sock is never closely inspected, easily hidden in its partner, and if necessary, very easily thrown away. So the washing machine fairy doesn't steal socks, legions of lost wank socks are gathered in rigid, crusty clans in landfills the world over...men really are disgusting.

Now it's time for the confession, I circulate my socks. I wash them after every usage, and they are never used twice before washing. So, when my mixed fibre M&S blue tartan sock— number four in a cycle of five went missing, I noticed. I was more than mildly concerned when its partner went missing but when an orange tartan sock, five in a series of five, also went missing, two days later, I was perplexed.

The next evening, I came home to find my front door unlocked—I never leave my door unlocked, never. I check it three times before I walk to the car, always, I have to, it's my routine. On the next morning I made doubly sure the door was locked—six checks—but again found it unlocked on my return that evening. Nothing was missing, nothing moved, nothing out of place except, the socks, the tartan socks were gone.

Now if we put men and their normal but unpleasant drives to one-side—and it has to be accepted there are some very weird people out there—but who would steal a wank sock? On a sliding scale of nasty weird things to do, that's pretty high. Who could want an abused sock? Master criminals in need of innocent DNA? The thought did cross my mind at some disturbed hour of the night, but there's only one way to deal with paranoia, find proof. So, I got busy. I dressed for work and then systematically went from room to room gluing strands of hair between each door and its frame—yes, a touch OCD—it has been said before. I then locked up, glued another hair trap to that door and went to work.

I came home to find the door unlocked and yet not one single hair was broken. Had the intruders got wise to my scheme? Why unlock a door if you don't intend to use it? That evening I ordered a home security motion sensor detector with two cameras. It arrived three days later and in the interim period I maintained my hair trap regime—all to no effect. I fitted the camera system on the Saturday, and then decided to abandon my house overnight and not return until Sunday evening, giving the intruders plenty of opportunity to break-in. My Sunday evening viewing was as dull as Sunday evening viewing always is, there was nothing on, even though the front door was unlocked. I spent that night fitting a new lock and calling myself a fool for not considering mechanical failure before then—a new lock is so much cheaper than a video security system. I'd decided to give my plan another go. I left for work Monday morning and didn't go home till Tuesday night. I even left the door unlocked this time. I arrived home at ten o'clock Tuesday night to find the door was now locked, locked but the house and motion sensors were undisturbed. I felt as if I was being toyed with, purposefully provoked, it was infuriating. The next day I called in sick, locked the door and drove around the corner. An hour later I sneaked back on foot and hid in the hedge that surrounds my garden. I had a good view of the front door and was determined to stick the day out. I was going to discover who my tormentors were and have it out with them—but come five thirty, my usual time to return home, I'd seen no-one but the postman. I was cold, dejected, stiff and sore and had been bitten to itchy distraction by midges—also in desperate need of the toilet. I stepped out of my hiding place, put my hand on the door handle and the bloody thing was unlocked. It wasn't possible, it was bloody impossible, and then the irrational thought elbowed its way through my frustration and past all my reasoned safeguards... ghosts.

I have a problem with ghost stories, or to be more exact those who tell them. For example—Fred Nibs claims to have witnessed some ghostly / magical / alien / miraculous happening and then adds the all-telling adjunct, "I've never seen anything like it!" Which is an assertion of authority, "I'm an experienced wise person and therefore, as this is outside my field of experience it must be something ghostly / magical / alien / miraculous." However, what it really means is, "I think I am a lot smarter than I am and as I can't explain this, it must be ghostly / magical / alien / miraculous." All religions, superstitions and cults are built on this very human weakness, and I despise such things, or at least I did.

As soon as the errant idea bruised its way in, I rejected it, and called myself daft for thinking such things. I threw off my clothes and jumped into the shower. I set it to its most narrow and pummelling setting, cranked the heat up all the way and stood there until the knots in my calves eased and the bites on my neck numbed. Then I wrapped a towel around my waist and stepped back into the kitchen—to find a woman dressed in a tartan coloured bustle and hoop skirt standing at my kitchen sink.

"I think these things are marvellous, hot, cold, hot, cold. In my day we had to heat up pails on the stove, back and forth, back and forth all day long, it's a wonder I wasn't scalded..."

"Who are you and what are you doing in my house?" I demanded but as soon as the words had left my mouth, I knew what she was, because as real and formed as she seemed, in her dark tartan dress and tidy white piny, she was not solid. I could almost see through her; it was like looking through a distorted stained glass.

"I don't rightly know pet?" Despite her lack of substance, her voice was clear, light and cheery and did not seem at all concerned by her own admission of amnesia. "I can remember chores and the names of things and stuff, like this is a sink and that's a stove although not like the one we had.

I remember Camp Coffee and Oxo but not me own name, odd ain't it."

"You're a ghost."

"Am I? Well I suppose I must be at that. Don't feel like a ghost. But how should a ghost feel ah? Knighted if I should know," she paused and then set the tap to run fast, placing her hand under the gushing water. At first it passed through her hand and then as her eyes narrowed, the water splashed against her palm and sprayed her face. "Look at that, now that's something...things is changing all the time now."

"Why are you here?"

She turned off the taps and turned to face me squarely, "can't say there's any reason why, I think I used to live here."

"Did you die here?"

"I can't rightly say, don't remember dying at all but it stands to reason I must have right. Can't be a ghost if you're not dead. Would you like a cup of tea duck?"

"Sorry?"

"Nice cup of tea. Best thing for a shock. You go get yourself comfy and I'll fix you a nice cup of tea. To tell the truth I've been dying to have a go at that new-fangled kettle there for ages. Go sit yourself down and I'll bring it in to you."

It may seem a little odd that I did exactly as the ghost bid, but what else could I have done? Run out of the house wrapped in a wet towel, yelling, "There's a ghost in my house making tea!" I can imagine how that would have ended, with yours truly locked up in the funny farm. So, I took my dressing gown from its hanger, pulled it tightly around the towel and myself and made my way into my small square dining room. I sat there listening to the kettle boil and the tink of teacups being taken from the cupboard and placed on a tray by a spectral maid—all the time wondering, "how far from the funny farm am I?"

"I love these tea pouches, very handy," the ghost's singsong voice rang out.

"Teabags we call them teabags."

"Amazing really, paper that doesn't fall apart in hot water, amazing. You don't take sugar, do you?" She floated into the room, tray in hand, and set it before me. My single service teapot, cup and saucer and a small measuring jug half filled with milk alongside a small plate neatly arranged with ginger biscuits. "Never seen you take sugar, but they say it's good for a shock so if you want some."

"No, no thank you. This looks very nice." I heard myself say and then thought better of it. "I'm sorry but you're a ghost and you've just made me tea. This is all a bit odd and how come you know I don't take sugar, and you said you wanted to use the kettle and the stove...you've been watching me."

"Course I 'ave; just 'cause you can't see me don't mean I can't see you. I've been watching you a lot," she smirked. If it's not possible for a bloodless creature to blush, then she did a pretty good job of faking it.

I however had plenty of blood in my system and turned bright red, "When? When have you been watching me?"

The ghost giggled.

"It's not like I went out of my way to watch. You didn't exactly hide yourself, yanking on ya thingy?"

"Why should I? This is my house, my thingy!"

"Your house. I've been here longer than you have. I've been dusting for as long as I can remember. I've been damp dusting so long the dust don't notice me no more. But I keep on doing it. I just keep going because...the devil makes work for idle hands don't he. I never knew what that meant but it sounded bad, so I kept busy. I think I'd have gone funny in the head if I hadn't been so busy, and then you turn up, and I kind of liked the look of you and then I saw you and your idle hands...well it looked a lot more fun than I'd been led to believe."

"Does privacy mean nothing to you?"

The ghost shrugged, "not much,"

I poured myself a cup of tea and considered the situation. It was six o'clock in the evening and I was sitting down to have a cup of tea with a ghost, a newly sexually enlightened ghost at that—I'm not sure I've ever had an odder day. I sipped my tea; it was very good.

"So, if what you say is true."

"I'm no liar!" Her surface darkened like a storm cloud.

"I mean to say, if what you say is accurate, you're been dusting unnoticed for what? At least a hundred years probably more, judging by that dress. But in this last week you've been unlocking and locking my front door and now you're making me tea, so tell me...what do you want?"

"I just want to...to be," the ghost sighed. Her colour lightening as she bowed her head and straightened her skirt.

"To be?" I answered, "what is this Hamlet?" She shifted in contrast and sharpness under my glare. The perfect lines of the tartan stripe were the only constant and straight thing about her form, "and how do you propose, to be?"

"All I need is some fresh, you know...whatchamacallit."

"Whatchamamacallit?" There was something about that skirt, I just couldn't place.

"You know, missions. I need more of your missions."

"Missions, do I look like Tom Cruise? What are you talking about?" That Bloody skirt, it really had me distracted, I knew I'd seen it somewhere. "What whatchamacallit missions...do you mean, emissions!? You need my emissions."

"I do Sir yes."

"You stole my wank sock! You're wearing my wank sock!"

The ghost maid slid briskly to the other side of the room, "So? You'd finished with it, so I possessed it."

"You possessed my wank sock. How dare you? How many? Tell me how many of my socks you possessed."

"I ate some of them."

"Unbelievable, the bloody nerve of it."

"And here I am. It's like magic."

"It's a bloody liberty."

I think you'd agree I'd done a pretty good job of holding it together up to that point. "This is outrageous! You've invaded my privacy, my personal space and...and ...I feel violated! And you want more, I not having this, get out! Get out at once, go on fuck off!"

"I don't see why you're getting so upset, it don't cost you nuffin'."

"Out! Get out of my house!"

The ghost stamped a formless and soundless foot and declared, "You selfish git. You just wait you...we'll see about this!" and disappeared with a dry snapping tut.

Now was I mad or not? I needed to know. I straightened the teacup on its saucer and took in the scene. Tea had most certainly been made and set, and yet I was sure I had not set it. I'd drunk half a cup and yes, I was still wearing my dressing gown and a damp towel. The room was empty. There was no ghostly apparition to be seen, no faint ghostly light, no chill in the air, no smell of sulphur and yet I was sure a ghost had been there. I finished the cup of tea; it was still warm. Could a man be mad and yet so calm? I think not, which meant...I'd just had tea with a ghost.

I set about searching the house, for what I am not sure, but I knew I had to do something, and a search was the thing to do. Every cupboard and nook, every draw and shadow and I found exactly what I expected, nothing. The kitchen floor was still wet with spray and the tea set still had to be washed-up but apart from that, there was no evidence the ghost maid had ever been there at all. I left all the lights on that night, but I still didn't sleep well.

I awoke unrested and sore and unpleasantly stiff, to find

a breakfast tray beside me. Toast, a jar of marmalade, orange juice, tea and one freshly cut flower. I was sorely tempted but I thought better of it and quickly got dressed and left the house. I didn't bother to lock the front door. As you can imagine I spent a rather distracted day at work, a lot of time spent on the internet looking up hauntings and exorcisms. and erotic ghosts—which threw up some very odd stuff—I also stumbled upon the term Homunculus—a very weird Renascence idea that life could be created by fermenting horse manure and human semen—perhaps I should have been glad the ghost hadn't brought a horse into my house.

I returned home to find a loaf of fresh bread had been baked and the table set with cheese, pickles and a slice of ham. I threw it all in the bin and threw a microwave meal into the machine and sulked for the full four minutes it took to become something wholly unlike the picture on the packaging. My meal was accompanied by a continuous bodiless, "tut tut tut."

This went on for a week, I'd wake up to breakfast and come home to simple but fresh food and I ignored it all. I never tasted a crumb of it. Food was not the only pleasure I decided to cut back on. I reasoned that if I starved the ghost of the source of its power it would eventually fade back into the background and after ten days of abstinence, I thought I'd proved my theory—because on the eleventh morning there was no breakfast and that evening there was no food at all. I waited a full three days before...well before the need, outweighed my caution. It had been a busy, perhaps even mental, couple of weeks and I was tired, and I needed to sleep. Look I'm not going to make any excuses, I was tired and I needed to relax enough to sleep, so I took the situation in hand—so to speak—and was approaching the point of fulfilment, and grabbed the nearest thing to hand, a pair of used briefs. I was quickly approaching the point of no return when I heard a giggle—the bedcovers flew off, the briefs were wrenched away and before I could do anything about it I had delivered a full load into the grinning spectral face of a long dead maid.

"Oh, you baggage! Get off me! Get off me!"

"Thank you, Sir, don't mind if I do."

"Get out!"

I ran downstairs full of wrath and heat and ready to roar— and there she was, a life size, lifeless, Art Deco nude sitting cross legged on my dining room table. Grinning like a loon and as cool and pale as porcelain. She fixed her translucent colourless eyes on me and began singing.

"Oh! Mister Porter, what shall I do?

I want to go to Birmingham and they're taking me on to Crewe.

Send me back to London as quickly as you can.

Oh! Mister Porter, what a silly girl I am."

Until that moment I hadn't felt any fear but seeing her living and yet lifeless form perched and pert did it for me. My back was up against the wall and my heart was beating the retreat my legs weren't strong enough to obey.

"What do you want?"

"You know what I want."

"No more, I won't you can't make me."

In one smooth easy movement she slid off the table and pressed her cold, chilling breasts against my chest, "Silly boy, you can't help yourself, you know that. All I've got to do is wait. I'm good at waiting. I could wait in your room, in your bed, in your sock drawer and you'd never even know I was there. Why not just feast your eyeballs and have a go, you know you want to."

"But I don't, you can't make me...it won't happen."

"Need a little help do we...?" An icy fist grabbed my crotch and tightened its grip.

"That's not going to do it."

"So, what will?"

"A pulse...and a dick."

She stood back, hands on her alabaster hips and scowled, "Do what?"

"I'm gay you silly, silly ghost girl thing. Gay and I don't mean happy."

"Gay?" the baffled ghost was suddenly dressed in her tartan frock and looking very perplexed.

"You're dead dear and having sex with dead people is a very strange place I don't want to visit. Secondly, I don't like girls, I like men, so even if you were alive, you'd still have places I wouldn't want to visit. Do you understand?"

"You're a nancy?"

"Yes, and thank you so much, for that touch of authentic Victorian bigotry. So, you can just shut up shop, point those things elsewhere and bugger off."

Her whole form trembled and then quivered and bubbled like boiling porridge. She fell to the floor and wept waterless tears, howling a high-pitched cry of dark, bottomless desperation. I'd never heard anything like it, but I recognised the emotions, I recognised the desperation. It was a cry of loss, grief unbound. I knelt beside her, held my breath and then held her hand, her ice sculpture hand.

"I just want to live."

"I know, I'm sorry. I'm sorry I can't help."

"It's not your fault. You never brought anybody home... how was I to know?"

"No, well there are reasons for that. Things have changed a lot since your day. I was married to another man, Simon, he died. I don't want to go through that again and I don't want to put anybody else through it. Simon and I shared a condition."

"Are you ailing?"

"No, I'm doing very well, because I look after myself and keep myself healthy...I find it helps if I keep everything around me clean."

"You do clean a lot."

"Yes, I suppose I do. I like it, so you see I really don't want a woman or need a housemaid."

Her tartan frock shimmered and darkened, "who are you calling a housemaid?"

"Well I just presumed, you said you did the dusting."

"Only to keep busy. I've got a trade I have."

"A cook?"

"Bleedin' men, you haven't changed that much then, I'm no housemaid I'm a seamstress."

"A seamstress really, you make dresses," I pointed to her current twinkling tartan affair.

"Of course, but anything really. I'm as good as any bloody tailor you care to mention, I'll tell you that much for nuthin'."

Now you can call me mercenary if you want to, but I know a gift horse when it materialises in my dining room. A Homunculus may be a ridiculous idea but perhaps sometimes, like flowers, ideas need a shitty start, and it's what you do with that shitty start that matters.

"And what do you do Mr.?"

"I was in marketing, but I always fancied myself as a bit of a...You need a beard."

"I need a what?"

"A front, someone whose presence gives you the appearance of...normality. And perhaps, so do I?"

"I've just remembered my name is Myrtle."

"I can see why you'd forget that. I have a proposition...if I make certain deposits, indirect deposits into your bank... would you be willing to make certain deposits into my bank."

"How do you mean like?"

"Myrtle, you're going to be. And be very, very busy."
"I'd like that..."

"Hare House Fashions" was born that day and we—Myrtle and I—are doing very well thank you very much. I feed her need and she helps me to be independent and in control. She makes really lovely period garments and I manage the distribution, advertising and the warehouse. We have a lovely range of 'Little Princess Costumes' and you've probably seen her dresses on T.V, the BBC depend on us. We're really very reasonable and very efficient and Myrtle's work is always, always top notch. We don't make a fortune, but Myrtle and I don't need a lot, we have each other and our routines—we get by, by lending each other a hand...on a regular basis.

# MR. HEDGES

"Whatever is the matter dear?" asked Mrs Briggs, a woman with the figure of a badger and a widow's eye for grief.

The wet eyed young woman standing on her doorstep whimpered, "Toothache," whilst holding her face. "I've been up all night. It hurts so much. It's driving me mad and I can't find a dentist."

Mrs Briggs had only met Evelyn once before, on the morning the removal van had deposited the young woman at the adjoining cottage. She's introduced herself to Mrs Briggs as soon as the van had left. An act of old-fashioned politeness, that wasn't wasted on the village's stout matriarch. And so, it was, with great enthusiasm that Mrs Briggs set about setting things in order.

"Come on in dear. Now don't worry. We'll get you in with Mr. Hedges, a fine man, semi-retired but he still keeps his regulars. I'm sure I can get him to see you. He used to be one of my late husband's customers." The number was dialled.

"Hello Jane, it's Iris here dear. Yes, fine thank you, bearing up. Now look Jane, I'd like to make an appointment for a friend of mine...Evelyn. Yes, my neighbour. Yes as soon as possible please. Marvellous, oh yes, I can vouch for her. I'm sure she can keep a secret. Thank you, Jane, see you soon." The receiver was replaced.

"There you go, all sorted. We can pop round as soon as you're ready."

"Thank you. Secret? You said I can keep a secret," Evelyn asked with a furrowed brow.

"As I said dear, Mr. Hedges is semi-retired. He likes to keep his business dealings quiet. We usually work on a barter system but if you have any money handy, I'm sure that will be fine. Is that a problem?" Mrs Briggs asked, staring sternly over the silvered rim of her bifocals.

"No not at all. Thank you, thank you so..." A blast of pain shot through Evelyn's head and ricocheted all the way down to her feet, "Jesus!"

"Oh dear. Have you taken anything for it?" Mrs Briggs asked peering into her handbag.

Evelyn nodded—she had in fact tried a wide and varied range of analgesics and alcohol, all to no effect.

"Well never mind, soon be over, it's just round the corner. I'll walk you there myself." Mrs Briggs stood to go.

"I'm sorry. It's stupid I know but..." A fresh torrent of shame and tears welled up inside her, "I'm scared of dentists."

Mrs Briggs placed a calming hand on her arm and smiled, "Don't worry about that, I have something here that will help." Two pink pills were removed from her handbag and placed in Evelyn's tremulous hand. "Take these now and by the time you get there you'll feel as right as rain, without a care in the world."

Evelyn hurried to her kitchen, filled a glass with whiskey and swallowed the pills down—the whiskey so enraged her tooth her she almost screamed.

They walked briskly through the village, the elder leading the younger, talking brightly as she shared tiny snippets of village history. A king slept there. A witch was drowned there and the only bomb we saw in the whole of the war fell there. Evelyn was not the slightest bit interested but was grateful for the distraction and tried her best to make as many encouraging noises as her mouth would allow.

"Here we are then," Mrs Briggs announced cheerily. They'd come to attention outside a thin, shabby, Victorian house with grey windows. Evelyn inspected the flaking building closely. There was nothing about it to suggest it held a professional or successful dental practise. No brass name plate. No new Mercedes in the drive. Not very promising.

"You are coming in with me. Aren't you?"

"Yes of course dear, if that's what you want."

Evelyn nodded firmly.

A tiny, bow-backed woman dressed in a floral apron and a long sleeved, threadbare black dress opened the door.

"Jane darling this is Evelyn," Mrs Briggs sang out.

Jane silently bowed as much as her curved back would allow her and then led them through a panelled door into a tiny, airless room. Three heavy wooden chairs crowded around a worn, faded rug and a mass of long-dead flies. Evelyn felt dizzy. She rushed to the room's only window and peered through the cobweb-laden panes. Outside the twisted branches of an ancient Yew tree gloated over the worn headstones of the church cemetery. She was not greatly comforted.

Jane took hold of her arm and led her across the crunching carpet of dead flies to another door. Evelyn waved a nervous goodbye to Mrs Briggs, who responded stout-heartedly with a show of crossed fingers.

Tottering on her tiny feet the rigid old woman led Evelyn into a room designed by her nightmares. Centre stage was the chair, a black leather-tilting chair, with a wooden headrest and a worn wooden footboard. Above it loomed a freestanding disc light, as bent and buckled as Jane—and just as dusty. The room looked as if it doubled up as a junk room, the shelves were crowded with clocks and jars and glass cases—some of which were occupied by disintegrating stuffed birds and forever startled stuffed rodents.

Leaning against the chair was an old battered metal trolley which held the remnants of an old bicycle or perhaps it was a long redundant sowing machine, "Why have a bicycle in a dentists?" Evelyn asked grey Jane. Who smiled sympathetically as she guided her towards the chair.

Evelyn's eye fixed upon a row grey metal implements. The very instruments of torture themselves. They did not shine or glint but lay dull and heavy on their trolley like shards of dirty ice. Evelyn giggled and covered her face with her hands. The old woman patted her back gently. Jane's bony hand worked its way carefully down Evelyn's back in slow, firm circles until it rested at the base of her spine and then, with a steady but firm pressure she pushed Evelyn's hip sideways— Evelyn fell into the sighing leather.

The ceiling was wrapped in cobwebs. It occurred to Evelyn that this was not a good thing. Not a good thing at all but she couldn't work out why? She tried to turn her head to question her aged guide, but her head resisted her. She couldn't move. A strange sensation was creeping up her legs, a warm numbness—she couldn't feel her feet. There they were, poking out of the bottom of her black slacks but they were utterly numb and totally unresponsive to her will, they would not move.

"I think I may have overdosed," she smiled, as the warm, sodden duvet of dope, enfolded her.

"I haven't felt this relaxed in years," it was a miracle. She was no longer afraid. "So...where's the dentist? Bring it on."

The floor at her side creaked. From the corner of her stupefied eye Evelyn could see a trapdoor slowly opening. It rose to its highest point and then fell, landing with a thud against the base of the chair, leaving the dark cavity of the basement exposed. A thin wooden ladder protruded into the room. Evelyn watch grinning and mesmerised.

The smell of sour fridges wafted into the room, as the sound of creaking leather shoes and rasping barber straps echoed beneath her. Gradually the scent of butcher shops and the stink of tinned corned beef intensified, saturating the air, as a corpse the colour of spoiled pork, crawled out of the pit.

It stood before her swaying on its emaciated heels. Its face no more than a sagging mass of meat held in place by thick strands of pale knotted string. Evelyn's scream withered in her throat.

Its arm reached out across the room in a stiff wide arc, moving first over the metal trolley, then across her waist, over her breasts and towards her throat. It took hold of her jaw. Forcing it open with a sharp squeeze. The rank skinned fingers slid like sandpaper across her lips and into her mouth, grating like sandpaper as they moved along her gums.

His smell scoured Evelyn's throat and braised her eyes, but she couldn't shut them. She couldn't move. She stared fixedly forward into the putrid face, as the milk-white balls slopped about in Mr. Hedges ragged eye sockets.

The metal trolley suddenly rattled and a moment later an unseen metal probe clicked against her teeth. Evelyn wanted to scream. She really, really wanted to scream. To scream and run away and scream herself dumb, but not one muscle would obey her. She was riveted to the chair, rendered helpless by terror and dope, a wide-eyed witness to every rotting crease and crevice in Mr. Hedges decaying face.

A dry flake of skin floated down from his mottled brow. She just knew it was going to land in her mouth—it tumbled through his eyebrow, along his twisted nose and then vanished from view. But she felt it land. She tasted it. She wanted to be sick. She needed to vomit. Her body was already in spasm but could she risk being sick? What if she choked? Somebody would have to help her if she were sick. Surely, he'd have to stop if she were sick! Mr. Hedges snapped her mouth shut and squeezed her nose with a deft pinch. She swallowed.

Creaking like the deck of an old boat he turned away from her, picked another instrument from the trolley and then swung laboriously back with the groan of aging ropes.

Evelyn squeezed her lips tight together but again the fingers forced her mouth open and crept inside. A large metal cylinder flashed before her, shifting in size and shape as it moved closer. Evelyn's weeping eyes managed to focus for a moment. It was a thick metal needle screwed into a syringe. The galvanised scorpion stung her pallet twice. At last the dead hands loosened their grip.

The corpse stood before her, fixed to the spot, its jaw open upon its withered chest, its dead eyes staring back into its own skull, motionless. The tiny grey crown of Jane's head bobbed into view above the corpse's right shoulder and then disappeared below it. Evelyn heard an odd mechanical whirr, as if a dry wheeled treadle were being forced into life and then Jane's head appeared again and the whirring grew louder and faster and again the old lady's head appeared and disappeared and the whirring intensified.

A gyrating drill trilled roughly in the corpse's hand. Mr. Hedges drove his empty hand into Evelyn's mouth and wedged it open with his bony knuckles. The drill moved inside, clattering, clattering against her teeth.

Evelyn awoke, her head was full of the taste of cloves. For a moment Evelyn had the impression she was watching herself move, as if her senses were somehow lagging behind her body. She caught up with herself on the edge of the dentist's chair. Leaning forward, she eased herself up and out of the chair. She didn't topple over. Panic pricked her heels and she jumped across the room and fled through the door before she'd even taken another breath.

Mrs Briggs sat in the waiting room, an empty cup and saucer perched on her knee, "Hello dear, all done?"

Evelyn gasped for breath, her pounding heart intent on blocking her windpipe.

"Jane asked if you'd mind paying in kind. I told her that would be fine. She left a shopping list, just a few groceries really."

Evelyn stared at her, madly sucking in air.

"There's no hurry you could drop them off tomorrow."

"Dead," Evelyn panted.

Mrs Briggs nodded perfunctorily.

"Dead!" Evelyn yelled.

"Yes dear. For years now, just before I married Mr. Briggs."

"You knew!"

"Of course."

"But how?"

Mrs Briggs placed the cup and saucer on the chair beside her, "Well, you see I went to school with Jane, Miss Hedges, we've been friends ever since, so when Mr. Hedges died we helped Jane out."

"He touched me! My god the smell!"

"Yes, I know, embalming was never my Joseph's strong point," Mrs Briggs stood and straightened her skirt. "That's why I gave you the pills darling. We all use them, such a shame." Mrs Briggs smiled as she handed Evelyn the shopping list, "Not a word to Jane now, she's rather sensitive about it."

"It was horrible," Evelyn wept.

"Oh, come on, it wasn't as bad as all that was it?"

"Yes! Yes, it was!" Evelyn shouted, "a dead man put his hand in my mouth!"

"Yes dear, but how is your tooth?"

Evelyn had forgotten the tooth, she felt for the thing with

her tongue, it was still there, she bit down hard but nothing happened. She prodded the molar with her finger, no pain, no discomfort. Not even the slightest soreness remained.

"It's fine."

"Well there you go."

"But the dentist is dead!" Evelyn insisted.

Mrs Briggs took her arm and cradled the young girl's hand in her own, as she led her out of the surgery. "Yes, dear he is, but that's our little secret. We wouldn't want to lose him, would we? After all, a good English dentist is so hard to find these days."

# RESTITUTE

*For Eliza*

As many children know but all adults seem to have forgotten, the devil lives down the toilet. You can hear his voice behind the roar of the flush. His realm dwells behind that kink at the back of the toilet. The "U" bend is the only thing that stops the devil reaching up and grabbing your bum when you're trying to do what you have to do.

Children are assured that this unquestionable truth is not so, pure nonsense. And as soon as they become adults, they accept the lie. Of course, it's nonsense, what a silly thing to think. We even tell their children it isn't so. Life is very strange. But the devil does live down there, way down past the wiggly bit, way down along the long dark pipes, in the dark sewage filled tunnels where men hardly ever go—think about it, all our wisdom and fear of evil lost and forgotten, because of our trust in sanitation, for shame.

Then again perhaps it's for the best, after all you can't spend your life worrying about the devil biting your bum. And of course, that's the best place for him, out of the way where he can't do any real harm. But just because he's down there doesn't mean he likes it, and just because we've forgotten him doesn't mean he's forgotten us.

Marcus B. Newt was playing in the lane behind his mother's house when a large orange tractor rumbled into the nearby field. It was pulling a plump, bright green eight-wheeled cylinder behind it. Marcus ran to his favourite tree, a thick crinkled oak with perfectly spaced branches, and climbed to its very top with speed and ease. From his vantage point Marcus watched the tractor work its way back-and-forth across the muddy, ridged field as its spinning mechanical arms. threw plumes of black sludge out into the air.

The smell was brilliantly awful. Sickly sweet and yet rotten and foul beyond belief. It smelt so bad it made Marcus' eyes water and his head hurt. He very nearly fell out of the tree.

"This," Marcus gagged, "this is why I hate the countryside, it bloody stinks."

Yes, Marcus loved climbing trees, but he climbed walls and monkey-bar climbing frames in the city parks just as well. Yes, the countryside had birds and animals, but city parks were full of pigeons and ducks and some even had squirrels. Then there were the wolves in Battersea—nobody at his new school believed him when he told them about the wolves—but what did they know, bloody country bumpkins. Yes, the city had its stinks too but at least in the city you could hide from them, shut the door on them, go in or go out and have pizza and avoid them. Not in the countryside, in the countryside you were stuck with the stink and it was likely to follow you around all day long—he was sick of it.

Marcus couldn't take the smell anymore, and it was getting late. He climbed down, dropping from the last branch he caught his arm on a bush with a deep green, spear shaped leaf. His arm stung. He grabbed at the bush and snapped a handful off. The centre was filled with a soft white, spongy substance. He turned his heel to it and kicked until the whole bush was shredded and shattered and lay discarded torn from the ground. This done he ran home with one hand over his nose and mouth.

The sound of a TV gameshow was blasting out from the front room.

"Is that you Marcus?"

"Yes Mum," who the bleedin' else was it gonna be?

"Take your shoes off."

"Yes Mum," give it a rest woman.

"You'll have to fix yourself something, they've offered me some extra hours at work."

"Okay Mum," peanut butter sandwiches and crisps it is then.

"What is that stink?"

"They've put shit on the field."

"Language thank you. Manure is the word."

"Stinks like shit."

"It sure does honey. They ought to warn people before they do that. Will you be alright on your own?"

"Yes Mum," like it would make any difference.

Peanut butter and strawberry jam sandwiches for tea, not that Marcus really minded, at least with Mum out of the way he didn't have to chow down on vegetables. Bloody vegetables—nothing good ever came from the countryside.

Marcus promised his Mum he wouldn't open the door to strangers or go out again after she'd gone to work—where would he go? He waved her off, threw a DVD into the machine and then sat down with three bags of crisps, his peanut butter and jam sandwich and a can of coke to watch "The Witches," his favourite film. But no sooner had he bitten into the much anticipated sandwich than he discovered a horrible truth—

to smell is to taste, and taste is mostly smell—the sandwich tasted of black stinky sludge—even the crisps tasted of shit, how bad can a day be if even your crisps taste of shit.

Marcus tossed the food to the other end of the sofa, picked up the phone and dialled his Dad's number, which rang and rang and rang. As it had on every night for the last week. He threw the phone at his rancid sandwich and the plate smashed. He made an urgent, ardent wish. It was born of rage, rage against his luck, rage against the countryside and his Mum and his Dad and his Dad's new, happily single, happy city life! He raged against them all. He was caught in the middle of everybody else's lives and couldn't do anything about it. Marcus stomped up the stairs and into the bathroom. The toilet seat was down—just like his Mum liked it. He kicked the toilet. He heard his toe crunch and saw lights flare in his head. He slammed the seat down, up, down and screamed down the bowl.

Through tear filled eyes he watched the water in the bowl swirl and then elongate and tunnel. He grabbed the handle and flushed. And then the water ran and rushed and then briefly settled. The water began to spin round and round as it rose up the bowl, rising towards the rim, changing from clear to yellow to brown to black, rising up, higher and higher. Marcus jumped back from the spitting bowl and watched the thick stinking water flow over the rim and spill out across the floor. He didn't know what to do but he had to do something, standing on his tip-toes he stepped into the water and flushed the toilet again—a fountain erupted from the bowl, broke against the ceiling and came crashing down on top of him.

"Oh shit," Marcus spat and then a hairy matted arm reached out of the toilet.

A strong muscular, filth smeared hand gripped the side

of the toilet bowl and pressed down. The elbow then bent back on itself, lifted high and began pressing and pumping, levering whatever was beneath up through the confining, twisted, flooded pipes. Marcus watched, soaked and shaking as two gnarled and twisted horns rose above the rim. A head followed, an angular head with thick eyebrows and an arrow sharp chin, covered in a straggly wet beard. A second arm followed, found purchase on the rim and in one smooth movement the goat man lifted himself from the toilet bowl. It stood before Marcus, wet and dripping and stinking like a dirty wet dog, its slit, yellow eyes weighed Marcus up with a glance and pushed him aside.

Marcus watched the goat man's nimble hooved legs skip down the stairs and he was happy to watch him go, relieved to have the creature out of his sight and then he heard plates crashing in the kitchen. Part of him wanted to find a dark corner and hide, part of him wanted to run down the street screaming, but the braver part that wanted to see what the goat man was doing down in his Mum's kitchen.

It stood before the long fridge freezer with both doors open, carelessly searching through the shelves with one hand, whilst holding half an apple in the other.

"Who are you?" Marcus' tremulous voice crept from his lips.

The goat man turned to face him, bleated once and then slammed the fridge door shut. There was a pizza takeaway menu stuck to the door. The goat man ripped it off, sniffed it and then threw it into Marcus' face. It fell to the floor at his feet. The goat man stamped his foot and pointed to the menu.

"You want me to order food?"

The creature walked to the sink turned on the taps and stuck his horns under the running water.

"What do you want? What should I order?"

It ignored him, grabbed the washing-up liquid and poured it over its head.

"I don't have any money..." Marcus tried to explain to the shampooing goat man.

The jagged soapy head rose up from under the taps. The goat man fixed Marcus with a contemptuous glare, kicked a hoof backwards and snorted. Marcus collected the peanut butter smeared phone from the sofa and dialled.

A voice with chewing gum between its syllables answered, "Good Day Pizza, can I take your order please."

"Umm...placing an order please..."

"Delivery?"

"Umm...yes please."

"Okay so can I take your order please...what do you want?"

Marcus wondered and he thought, and then he looked through the doorway at the goat man, who had opened the washing machine and was sniffing a pair of his mother's knickers.

"I think, I want twelve large pizzas, two bottles of coke and three large tubs of coleslaw, better make that three bottles of coke."

Marcus gave the address and then came the question, "How are you going to pay?"

"Cash I guess."

The goat man walked into the room drying himself with one of Marcus' mother's dresses. He was taller than Marcus had first thought, so tall his horns were almost scrapping the ceiling, and he was muscular too, not like a body builder but more like one of those smack-down wrestlers he used to watch on TV with his Dad. His Dad would have said, "He looks a bit handy."

But it was the legs that Marcus couldn't look away from, thick legs, covered in a carpet of wavy thick hair, and they bent the wrong way.

"Are you the devil?" he asked. "Are you Satan?"

The creatures bleat was very clearly a laugh.

"If you were Satan...would you tell me? Would you hurt me?"

It threw the dress into Marcus' face and with a hop jumped up onto the back of the sofa and then summersaulted forward into the armchair. It then snapped up two bags of crisps and slammed them together with a clap of its hands. The crisps cascaded through the air and clung to his hairy chest. Marcus' shocked expression turned into a smile and then a laugh.

"That was great. If you're not the devil who are you?"

The goat man bleated, stretched out on the sofa and then kicked his legs into the air.

An image flashed into Marcus' head, a memory of something he'd seen in a book about a wardrobe, "You're a fawn..."

The beast sprang off the sofa and was nose to nose with Marcus, before he'd taken another breath. The beast's snake eyes narrow and burning.

"Not a fawn then..."

The creature stepped back and mimicked placing a crown on its head.

"A crown, you're a King...King of the fawns..."

The creature pointed up higher and higher still.

"Higher than a King, an Emperor, no—a god. You're a god."

The creature nodded.

A thought occurred to Marcus which he didn't bother to filter, "So why can't you speak English?"

"Because it's a fucking silly language." It snorted. "It

sounds like sheep bleating."

"That shouldn't be a problem for you?" Marcus observed.

"Do you see any wool boy?"

The doorbell rang. The goat man growled.

"It's the pizza guy. I don't have any money."

The goat god swaggered out of the room. Marcus heard the front door open, the delivery man screams, and then twelve pizza boxes, three bottles of coke and three large tubs of coleslaw were tossed back into the room, followed by a laughing goat god.

"Eat up boy, eat your fill."

"My name is Marcus not boy."

"And I am Pan, the Great God Pan, eat your pizza."

"I'm not hungry."

"Course you are. You need to eat. Keep strong and plump."

"Plump," Marcus sneered.

"Get meat on your bones boy, eat."

They ate and they laughed and the Great God Pan sang and told stories and whistled, and all with his mouth full of food, which he spat and sprayed all over himself and Marcus, and every corner of the room. Marcus couldn't remember ever having so much fun. And it was dangerous fun, which is the best kind of fun to have. He felt dangerous but unbeatable. As if he was climbing up to the very top of his favourite tree, knowing that when he reached the top, he was going to jump off—and keep on flying forever.

When the last pizza box was emptied, and the coleslaw tubs were licked clean Pan grabbed Marcus by the hand and pulled him to his feet.

"Time to go."

"Where are we going?"

"Out of here. To meet the Elder Mother, she lives in the city."

"You can take me back to the city?"

"A city."

"Will we be coming back?"

"Maybe, maybe not. Isn't half the fun not knowing?"

Marcus agreed it was and took Pan's offered hand and walked with him out of the house, into the field and...

Of course, Marcus' mother, Jan, was frantic, nearly driven mad with grief, guilt and shame. The pizza delivery boy told his story of the goat man monster that met him at the door, but no one really believed him, except Jan. The newspapers carried the story of the goat man, but they also told the world that Jan wasn't home because she had to work extra hours. They even told the world she worked extra hours because Marcus' father never paid maintenance, but people seemed to forget the facts as time passed. Rumours coagulated into lies and lies became the collective memory. Nobody seemed to remember the goat man, why would they, bound to be a villain in a costume. Nobody remembered she was a hardworking mother when the newspapers decided somebody had to be held account for her own loss.

It was late and Jan was sitting staring at the blank screen of the TV, when she heard a knock at the door—was it Marcus, home at last? She rushed to the door and opened it to find a short black woman standing on her doorstep. She wore a wraparound dress, a cosmically coloured statement of bold joy, her matching wraparound headscarf, a declaration of her inner confidence. Jan was immediately intimidated.

"Are you the mother of that lost boy?" the woman asked.

"I am," Jan replied, "and you are?"

The woman reached out and took Jan's hand. Her skin was radiant, dark and yet vibrant with life and so warm, hot water bottle hot, "I have come to return your son to you."

Jan's heart flipped, "where is he?"

"Do you know the Elder mother?"

"Do I know what?"

"The Elderberry tree is a holy tree and beloved by the Elder mother. It must be honoured; an offering must be made before it is cut. Your son showed her no respect and on her most holy of days..."

A mad woman. A mad black woman was standing on her doorstep talking nonsense, "Will you please go away."

"Restitute we must..."

"Please go!" She slammed the door shut.

Another knock on the door. Jan ripped it open to find a thin, spotty faced pizza delivery boy on her doorstep.

"Delivery," he beamed.

"I didn't order anything," she snapped looking down the street for the mad woman.

"I know, it's a gift. I'm to tell you," he read from a note, "this is our gift to you, sorry for all your woes."

"I don't want it. I'm not hungry."

"Course you are. You need to eat," the boy insisted, "get some meat on those bones."

Jan nodded and accepted the gift. She retreated inside and sat on the sofa. She flicked the TV on and found a gameshow. She opened the box. It smelt good. She ate greedily and with gusto. What was that meat? It was greasy, thick and rich on the tongue. The taste danced within her and warmed her spirit with its homely simplicity, so good, so good—she tore the taped receipt from the lid and lifted it to the light; "Curried Goat! Really curried goat, who on earth would send her curried goat." Unbelievable, totally unbelievable what some people will do.

# RUNNING MAN

I grew up in a new town, a hollow town, a space created for the slipshod souls of the London overspill. It was clean, well-organised and well set out, but it was also stale, grey and dull. That strange fizzing element called culture refused to get on the train and stayed at home in the Smoke. Not that culture wasn't wafted under our noses. The roads and rows of same as, same as houses were named after poets and writers but that was a close as culture ever dared to come.

I lived on Chaucer Close. Discovering that Chaucer was a writer—my parents had the Penguin edition with the funny looking guy in pointy shoes on the front cover—had a profound effect on me. It meant that poets were somehow important—they named streets after them—so writing had to be good right? They haven't named a street after me yet, but I keep looking for that story, the story to change things around.

My best friend for the last forty years is an artist—yes, the two arty kids from the estate stuck together—and he's had some level of success, London shows that kind of thing. His generosity enables us to get together on a regular basis and enjoy one or two rather good bottles of red wine—or a lot of very acceptable mid-priced red wines. We were embracing quantity not quality a few weeks ago when he asked, "Remember Running Man?"

"Of course. I know the full story."

"Wife died in a car crash, sent him loopy..."

"That's not the story."

"It's not? Go on then, you're dying to tell it," he said pouring us both another glass of mid-priced Shiraz.

When I said ours was a hollow town, I wasn't just speaking metaphorically. It was literally hollow at its core. The town centre was an enormous concrete platform suspended above a dual carriageway supported on all sides by a gigantic multi-storey carpark. Some cities are walled and have city gates, mine was encompassed by a concrete grey carpark with electric barriers, manned by the knights of the NCP. If you were to ask a native, they'd probably inform you that it's the largest carpark in Western Europe, and they'd be proud of it too. A town created out of nothing, a Spirograph doodle brought to life but hollow and empty at its soul. People need stories. The best we had, the tale we all shared was the epic tragedy of the Running Man.

His story was certainly well-known but perhaps not fully clarified. He'd been out with his family and a passing car, bus or truck had ploughed into his wife, daughter or son and they had been killed in front of his eyes. Ever since he'd been running to escape his pain. Through the seasons and through all weathers he ran, from early morning till long after they turned on the yellow streetlights. He ran from one end of town to the other and when his trainers fell apart, he ran barefoot until someone threw a new pair at him.

Shoes and much else was often thrown at him. I think it was his smell that people struggled with. It was a smell you could taste, a smell you could see rising off him as he approached. He was basically constructed of rancid chicken bones wrapped in elastic bands. He was a sight; his grey vest might once have been a dishrag. His sweat-stained poultry legs protruded from baggy shorts that had long forgotten their colour or purpose and had to be secured with a length of binding twine around his non-existent waist. This grey skeletal horror was topped with an almost square human head that was entirely covered in stubble and fixed with a permanent baffled grimace. The sound he made, his theme music, was a throat rasping pant followed by a yell, which might have been "You" or "Oi," followed by a dry, toneless, clunk as he brought his fleshless hands together.

The estates that supplied the shops with workers and consumers were arranged outside the grey castle walls, separated by a moat-like dual carriageway. But those clever social engineers had supplied a plethora of bridges, underpasses and footpaths that meant you never had to actually touch a road, you just went under or over. As all paths converged on the town the Running Man was provided with a continuous track; so no matter which direction you came from, at some point, morning, evening or night, you'd cross the Running Man's path.

I was crossing a bridge, probably pacing out a poem or some such teenage affectation, when I saw Running Man rattling towards me. I stepped to one side as he approached and as I did so half a brick clattered against the railings next to me and dropped to the road below. I looked up thinking he'd kicked it in my direction, only to see six cackling kids running up behind him pelting with stones. Most missed him and ended up coming in my direction or flew directly over the bridge, but a few good hits were had. I shouted something that questioned their parentage and then made to run towards them. They returned the insults but scarpered. Running Man stopped next to me, put his toothpick fingers to the back of his head and brought them back smeared with blood.

I probably said something like; "Jesus mate you okay," I definitely remember stepping forward and then jumping back in order to escape his movable stench.

Running Man nodded and proceeded to shuffle on the spot as if he was ready to take-off again.

"Maybe you should get that looked at..." I ventured.

He shook his skull in disagreement and stared past me. I stooped into his line of vision and instantly wished I hadn't. His eyes were bursting with fear. He was flight personified.

"Sorry for your loss," I heard myself saying.

"What's going on up there?" A fist of voices shook the bridge, "look at my fucking windscreen!"

I looked over the railing and saw a long line of cars backed up along the carriageway. At least three had smashed windscreens. The angry driver-trolls looked up and swore to eat me or do other things to my young body that would have ruined me for life. I turned to the Running Man and said the only thing I could say, "Run."

He went in one direction and I in the other. I didn't stop till I hit town. I bet he didn't stop till sundown. Less than a week later I saw him again, sweating up the threadbare field we called the park. I stepped into his path and began asking how his head was, but he just clapped, sidestepped and kept going. He didn't even break stride.

I moved away from the hollow town not long after that and sought out companionship, culture and that fine shining story that I still haven't found. When asked about my hometown, being a native son, I spoke about carparks, bridges and underpasses and of course the Running Man. I've told his story to strangers who'll never see him. I've told the story of the bridge on two different continents, and in countless pubs and every time its told, I'd see his eyes and wonder what I should have said to reach him, what words would have eased his fear?

"You've never told me that before," my friend nodded appreciatively pouring himself another glass.

"But that's not the story. Thing is he died about three months ago. The local paper did an article and you know what?"

"What?"

No children, no family, he never married. He was alone in the world. Turns out the entire town had colluded in a lie. We'd made something up and told it to one another for over thirty years. The council paid for his funeral. The cortege drove around the town, a lap of honour for Running Man— which is a sweet gesture as gestures go but the truth is no one knew his story, not while he was alive. Sure, we gave him a great backstory, but it wasn't true. It wasn't his story. It was a hollow lie. We just explained away his pain for our own benefit without trying to help him.

My friend looked at me as only friends dare to do and leant back in his chair, arms. crossed behind his head,

"So, what was his name?"

"I can't remember."

"There you go then, he is the Running Man. He's not dead. He's a myth now, greater than ever, beloved by all. They'll be telling his story for years. Whatever the truth, people will always prefer the myth. I wouldn't mind betting his ghost is running still...good story."

"Great story."

"You could write that story."

"Yeah, Running Man's biography within a ghost story. I like that...The Ghost Runner."

And I wrote it and I sold it for the price of a pizza, so not the story I was looking for after all.

# THE GREATEST SLIMMING PILL IN THE WORLD... EVER.

"It's simply the greatest slimming pill in the world...ever. In fact, I'd say it's going to be the defining product of the age. Any age."

"That's some sales pitch Mr. Johnson. You of course have something to back it up?"

"Twenty years of chemical analysis. It's all there in black and white."

A chorus of cleared throats rippled around the large oval desk as ten sets of fingers drummed across ten frighteningly thick document folders.

"Mr. Johnson do you know how many times a major drug company has taken up a product created by one single individual?"

"Isn't that tautology?"

"I beg your pardon?" The Chairman's indignation was nearly drowned out by his underling's collective sharp intake of breath.

"Sorry, I do that. I'm on the autistic spectrum...slightly. Kind of a light blue."

The chairman's eyebrows gradually lowered, "That would

explain your dedication to your project, but it doesn't prove its effectiveness."

"Indeed...the proof of the pudding is in the eating, which is kind of funny when you think that I'm trying to sell you a diet pill." A murmur of laughter fluttered across the room, only to be crushed into the thick pile carpet by the Chairman's well practiced scowl.

"This is a very serious business Mr. Johnson, and ultimately a business which intends to remain profitable."

"We both know the markets just sitting there. Getting fatter."

"One man's dedication to his own private obsession does not automatically create trust. Nor does it omit risk. In fact, it may very well increase it. No matter how well intentioned you are Mr. Johnson, there are a multitude of risks associated with bringing a new product onto the general market. Risks to investors and reputation."

"And clients," Mr. Johnson interjected with an elfish grin.

"...yes, and customers, which means lawsuits and loss. You may have given twenty years of your life to this project, but we don't want to have to pay for your mistakes twenty years down the line."

Johnson ran his forefinger down his narrow nose and then directed the same obstinate finger at the Chairman, "I think you've looked at my work and that's why I'm sitting here listening to your...cautious concerns. I welcome you to review my analysis and I'm confident that if you do, you'll agree this is the safest, most customer friendly product since nappy cream."

The Chairman picked up his folder and thumbed the pages, "obviously we've had an initial review, and yes that's why we're all here today. So, let's cut to the chase, here is our proposal. We will invest in your formula on these terms. and these terms. alone. Complete and total rights and ownership of the product."

Mr. Johnson's face paled. "I see. You expect me to sign my life's work, my chemical formula over to you?"

"If you want us to invest in eight years of research, yes. Our lawyers will make it sound a lot more complicated and watertight but essentially, that's the deal."

"And I get?"

"We can offer you a flat fee now with a second payment in eight years should the product prove to be marketable."

"Eight years, to discover what I've already proved."

"Eight years of research, tests and more tests and then trials and more trials. Eight years at our expense. That is the offer."

"I see…"

Five years later Mr. Gerald Johnson was handed a rather hefty pay cheque and "Subufree: The Greatest Slimming Pill the World has Ever Known!" Appeared on the market. Within six weeks it owned the market. How did it do it? To put it simply, canny marketing, that and it really worked. How did it do that, well I'm no biochemist but the marketing made it sound simple enough, but that's marketing for you. Simply put, you took one pill a day and just thought yourself thin. And that was the Marketing Department's main problem, it sounded too good to be true. This is the skimmed down version of the science; the brain is ninety percent fat, thoughts are energy that continually build new pathways or neurons, across the brain, made out of that fat. Mr. Johnson's pill simply allowed the brains ability to utilize fat to cross the blood brain accessing the body's other fatty deposits, which it broke down into amino acids which the body then treated as waste products. No, I don't believe it either but as I said it seemed to work, at least for a while.

The phone on Mr. Stainton's pale pine desk rang and a blue light flickered above the boldly displayed numbers. Ms. Droff was calling him. She wouldn't do that unless it was important. A fat finger with a well-manicured nail pressed the loudspeaker button.

"Yes Ms. Droff?"

"Sir, there's a Mr. Holland here to see you."

"Mr. Holland?" Stainton couldn't place the name although he knew he knew it.

"Yes Sir, he's second assistant, in the Subufree customer care department."

"Oh yes, scrawny looking guy. What does he want?"

To see you Sir."

"Does he need to be seen Ms. Droff?"

"I think so Sir."

Stainton trusted Ms. Droff's judgement, "Send him in then."

I shall summarize Mr. Holland's summery of the situation thus; "According to our research Subufree's potency can be enhanced by the customer. Basically, the happier the thought, the quicker the fat is broken down."

"And this data is coming from the feedback. Straight from the customers?"

"Yes Sir. It's trending all over the net. If you think happy this pill makes you thinner quicker."

"Incredible. Can we market this?" Stainton asked, although as soon the words left his mouth, he realized they'd been directed at someone far too junior to answer the question.

"Put a presentation together will you Holland, I'll let the people in marketing know it's coming."

Within six months the scarcity of Subufree on supermarket shelves was a hot topic, and worthy of discussion on news networks, and the subject of long-winded jokes by a multitude of stand-up comedians. It couldn't have sold quicker if it had been free. Production of three well-known antidepressants were halted in order to increase production to previously unheard-of amounts. Subufree was flying of the shelfs like a jet. People were fighting in Supermarkets for the new wonder drug. Subufree was indeed the greatest event of the age.

A year later, everybody had forgotten Mr. Johnson, mainly because no one had ever heard of Mr. Johnson. Outside of the ten businessmen, who'd all been sworn to secrecy about a highly confidential meeting in a conference room some years past, nobody knew it was his hard work and dedication that was behind the greatest event of the age. But had they known and had they been interested they would have seen Mr. Johnson change his name, empty his bank accounts and disappear from the world of men. To this day we don't know where he is—and by Christ we've looked for the bugger.

London Fashion Week, fourteen months after the launch of Subufree, who can forget it. The thrill, the style, the glamour and all the glorious, backbiting backstage.

"What does she think she looks like?"

"How very original..."

"Cow."

"She's spreads quicker than butter."

And then it happened, just as the pouting redhead with glacial skin strode elegantly down the catwalk—Boof! She was suddenly twelve pounds heavier and the weight wasn't evenly distributed either, it just appeared in mountains of bulbous mounds across her once picture-perfect body. There was no doubt about it the poor girl was suddenly large and ugly. The audience laughed as she lost her footing and toppled onto her now bouffant face. Boof—boof—boof! Suddenly ninety-seven percent of the audience were instantly ugly with a combined weight exceeding two tons.

Taunting teenagers were suddenly reduced to tears as—Boof—they became the owners of unbelievable levels of ugliness. Cyber bullies and trending Trolls felt their faces warp, their necks buckle and chairs collapse beneath their weight. Snide, bitter bridesmaids were struck down with shame and refused to get out of the cars that collected them. Resentful, pathetic men found their faces twisted into alien horror freak shows. Their faces broke mirrors at twenty paces, whilst their bodies grew so large, they couldn't reach their own belly buttons—let alone the women they once used to abuse to make themselves feel better. The American President, an African rebel leader and many religious leaders just exploded. Within twenty-four hours not only was the majority of the Western world morbidly obese, they were really, really bloody ugly. It took another forty-eight hours for the politicians to roll over, reach their phones and find someone with fingers thin enough to dial the numbers. The question asked in the British Parliament, across Europe and the American House of Representatives and Congress—all via blacked-out conference calls, for obvious reasons—what the fuck?

Stainton's girth encompassed the conference room's oval desk as more and more calls came in, demanding explanations for his product's unexpected side-effect. He had no explanation to offer and had to beg for time in order to investigate these, "unprecedented and challenging matters." But the politicians wanted answers and they wanted them quick, Stainton pointed out that such investigations were going to take some time as his company's shares were disintegrating; and only two percent of his workforce were able to face coming into work. They gave him seventy-two hours.

Oh, how the world groaned in those hours, how it mourned its lost beauty and grace, it was truly a time of testing and tribulation, the defining experience of the age.

Seventy-two hours later the Chairman Stainton broadcast his report to the world's leaders. I shall summarize, his summery thus—they'd been had.

"It would seem that the accumulative effect of consistent use of Subufree, broadens its effectiveness, in a sense its processes have not changed. It will still do what we said it will do. If you think thin, it will make you thin or indeed as has been shown, if you think happy thoughts you will be thin...but it seems. if you think ugly or unkind thoughts, the fatty deposits grow exponentially in the most inappropriate places....rendering the client ugly."

"And is this scenario reversible?"

"Can it be undone?"

"Is there a cure?"

The Chairman, raised his chubby hand and waited for the sobbing to end.

"It is obviously too early to be definitive in this matter, given time we may very well find a product to reverse these regrettable side-effects but at present, no. No, it seems. that any prolonged use of Subufree, let's say of over two months, renders the physiological changes permanent." Silence.

"However...as I said the effect, that is the beneficial effects of Subufree are still active...the only way, as we see it, to undo the potentially harmful or unpleasant effects of this product...is to use the product as it was intended."

"You mean to say, that if we want to lose weight and look...normal, we are going to have to think thin?"

"Normal is such an ugly word. I think, the only way to set this situation straight is to actively think nice thoughts. We have to be kinder to one another. If we want to be different, we have to be nice to one another."

"Doomed," someone whimpered.

But I'm not so sure, perhaps now that the threat isn't merely ecological or theoretical but is at last so very palpable; perhaps now we can get our house in order. Isn't it nice to think so? It is isn't it, nice, to think we can all, be a little nicer. I like to think so...and look, I've lost three pounds.

# STOCK TAKING

When was I was a sweaty lad, all bluster and no content, I carried a blade. A three-inch lock knife with a brass bolster. It was my safety blanket. I never left the house without it. Yes I was breaking the law but it made me feel safe, and that's what you did on my estate, you carried a blade just in case—just in case you crossed paths with another sweaty, blade blustering fool. I pulled it once, in a sixth form class when a toffee-nosed teacher dared suggest that working-class marriages were more likely to end in divorce. Being raised by your grandparents makes you sensitive to such things, and so ended my education.

Later that year Grandad Jack had a stroke. I spent the night by his bed watching him wither away. Jack loved two things—fags and cowboy books. So, I read to him, duel after duel, shootout after showdown. The shared flaw in the quick draw solution and my street-smart dumb thinking revealed themselves that night, so I swapped my knife for books and never went back.

I was hooked on books. I couldn't leave the house without a paperback. Any book would do, fiction, poetry, even plays. I couldn't get enough. I was mind expanding all over the place and the law couldn't touch me for it. But despite all the joy and wisdom I gleaned, I promise you, books caused me more hassle than my knife ever did.

One evening I was reading on the slow train from London when this suit with a glazed ham face said, "Where do you want to go?"

"Home," I replied.

"No, where do you want to go?"

"Basingstoke, next stop."

Pig hungry eyes narrowed as his ran a finger across my paperback, "Let's go somewhere private."

I checked the cover and then contemplated what reading, "The Complete Plays of Joe Orton," on public transport might suggest to others. "Nah...cheers mate, library book... got to look after it."

We finished the journey in awkward and possibly frustrated silence.

Then there was Fogg & Sons, a vast, echoing, corrugated steel warehouse with an ever-howling indoor wind, and an Alaskan chill factor. It stocked every kind of wire, cable, flex and connector known to mankind.

My working day entailed filling orders, climbing up ladders to get odds and sods and logging their departure. That and avoiding the ever-speeding red forklift that shifted coils of cable from one end of the warehouse to the other. Basic, go fetch, dogsbody work. Lunch was purgatory. Subjects included football, or football and girls, or how to do girls and football—so men sitting around swearing and lying to each other. I could do it. I knew how to play the sham but the book in my hand made other demands. Unfortunately, in such settings, reading in your lunchbreak was akin to carrying a vial of plague into a crèche. Utterly unforgivable. I couldn't have been more ostracised if I'd pissed in the tea machine and shat in the F.A cup.

"What you bring that in 'ere for then?"

"To read."

"Are you gay?"

I checked the cover, it wasn't Orton, "No."

"Posh Boy."

And that's how nick names are born. For the next six months, "Posh Boy" was my name.

Frank Fogg, known as Big Frank, ran the operation. An aggressive man of concrete opinions, there was no subject, no field of interest in which Big Frank didn't regard himself as an expert. He stated facts and those facts were not to be questioned. Truth be damned. If Big Frank said it was so, it better bloody be so. Frank once caught me reading "A Clergyman's Daughter" in my lunch break, "Dirty book Posh Boy?"

"Not really."

"Sounds dirty. What you reading for?"

"For?"

"Reading's not working."

He wasn't wrong but wasn't that the point. Two minutes later Frank bellowed; "Posh Boy, come 'ere." And I obeyed.

"Junction box. Rack five, fourth shelf," which meant, the top shelves, twenty-five feet up in the blue steel racking. I turned, searching the long narrow aisle for a ladder.

"No time for ladders Posh Boy," Frank jumped on the forklift and pointed to the truck's extended forks, "get on then, stop pissing about."

I got on. The electric engine whined and the forks shot up past the second shelf, past the third and the fourth, high into the roof space I went, and there I stayed. Forty foot in the air pinned against the thin aired ceiling. Frank whistled for his football loving brat pack and then led them in hurling rolled-up balls of packing tape at me, chanting, "No more reading! No more reading!" For half an hour.

Big Frank was a bully. An ape's arse of a man and yet—
and isn't it always the way—women loved Frank. I would like
to be able to qualify that statement by saying vulnerable or
inexperienced women or desperate lonely, hard-up, and ugly
women but I can't—the range and quality was too wide and
too numerous. Women were drawn to Frank. It was baffling, it
was depressing. Perhaps it was his look? Silvered hair, broad-
shouldered, the physique of a champion boxer with one last
big fight left in him. Perhaps it was his bulldog swagger or the
trigger-happy leer that comes from being an older man who
truly believes the word "no," doesn't apply to him. I have no
idea, but in they'd come—all summer dresses and high heels
with a smirk hidden behind their lipstick smiles to ask, "Is
Big Frank in?" And off to the office they'd go. An hour later
they'd leave, crumpled and ruffled with their lipstick sneer
wiped clean off their faces. We all knew, it wasn't even close
to being a secret. The in-joke went like this; "Where's Big
Frank at?"

"Getting himself some office action."

Not exactly funny but we'd all laugh, shake our heads
and wander into the chill warehouse wind, giving Frank's
office a wide birth until the unfathomable deed was done.
Nobody ever challenged him, nobody ever tried to put him
right. He was the boss and we didn't want to lose our jobs.
We were gutless, clueless, jealous boys, blinded by the loutish
manliness of Big Frank. I was no better but I did harbour
a sense of unease—I belief created by Anna Karenina's
misfortune—that these women, somewhere down the line
would be paying a hefty price for dealing with Big Frank, but
still they came.

It was the first Tuesday of the month and I was manning
the front desk with a concealed copy of Jack Kerouac's
"Doctor Sax," whilst Weasel—a skinny kid with constantly
blinking eyes and a ceaseless dry sniff—collected dead flies

from the front window display. I was doing my best to ignore his inane waffle about some football match that I, "Really, really shouldn't have missed." As I said "Aha," for the hundredth time the front door buzzer did its thing and a thinned lipped woman in a grey shapeless dress shuffled into the store. Definitely not a customer, we only ever served beer bellies with tattoos. She was a bit older than Frank's usual fare, but I decided I wasn't going to make it easy for her. I lowered myself down into Doctor Sax and waited for the magic words.

She stood there, head bowed, rocking from one dull shoe to the other, saying nothing for a whole minute. Feeling awkward I closed the book and smiled, "Can I help you?"

"Is Big Frank in?" she asked.

I'd never seen her before, never seen a photo and had no idea of her name, but I suddenly knew who she was, this was Big Frank's wife. It's the boss's wife and look what he's done. Something about her just broadcast boot heel and deep bruises. She'd once been one of those young, hot, Frank seeking girls and now she was Big Frank's wife—and she paid for it every day. She called him Big Frank, his own wife called him Big Frank. I looked into her eyes and felt the terrible cost of being Mrs Big Frank Fogg. Scorched by the realisation, I cast my question to Weasel, "Where is Big Frank?"

Without turning Weasel sniffed, "Getting himself some office action."

She didn't say a word, but I swear I saw her shrink. I looked away and stared at the counter and prayed for her to go. The door buzzer shrilled like a wasp and she was gone. Weasel's head appeared from the window display and looked about the shop.

"Who was that then?" he blinked.

"Salesman," I replied through a drying throat.

Frank strode in from the windy warehouse, his massive

bulk momentarily altering the room's gravity, "Who was that?" he demanded.

"Salesman," Weasel blinked.

"For what?"

Weasel looked at me with his furrowed rodent brow and sniffed.

"Soap Frank," I heard myself rasp.

"Soap, what the hell would I want with soap?"

"That's what I said Frank," Weasel chirped in, "I said, I said what do we want with soap mate. We does electrics, not soap right."

"Is that window done yet rat face?" Frank barked.

"Nearly," Weasel replied dropping down behind the display.

Frank turned to glare at me, reached across the counter and yanked the book from my fingers: "Told you Posh Boy, not on my time?"

"Just holding it Frank."

"Dr Sax, one letter out ah? Then it might be worth reading," he laughed as he dropped the paperback to the floor. "No more fucking reading," with his alpha male scent laid, Frank strode back into the warehouse and back into his office—which is where, being the first Tuesday of the month he should have been, where I knew he'd been all morning, checking on the stock. Why didn't I just answer the poor woman's question? Why did I ask Weasel? I knew when Big Frank found out I'd dropped him in it, I was done. Ten tons of kicking were coming my way, no doubt, no question, I was dead meat.

I lost sleep that night. I pictured Mrs Fogg freaking out, unable to keep her mouth shut and Frank shutting it for her with his boot. What had I done? What would he do to her? What would he do to me? What wouldn't he do? He'd wring me like a wet rag.

When I turned up the next morning the shutters were still closed. Weasel and the pack were yapping by the door.

"Frank hasn't turned up."

"He's late."

"Bet he's not coming."

My stomach winced. Was he in a Police cell? Was he on the run? Had he done her in with his bare hands? Had she stabbed him from behind with a pair of scissors? Was Mrs Big Frank staring white eyed at the inside of a morgue cabinet as we spoke?

"He'll have to pay, we've turned up," Weasel whinged.

"You be sure to tell him that," I snipped.

An hour later we were all still waiting like obedient pups when the manager of the neighbourhood bar, Frank's buddy, turned up to tell us to go home—Fogg & Sons wouldn't be opening today. No reason, no explanation, just not opening today.

Another disturbed night followed, why not leave town? Why not the country? I considered phoning in my resignation, who needs two weeks money? Would Big Frank still pay me? Would my broken fingers be able to grip the cash?

Thursday morning came and the shop was open. We all shuffled in without a word. I kept my head down till lunch time and then Weasel found me reading in the toilet, "Big Frank wants to see you now."

Into the valley of death went the one, totally prepared for a kicking, "Yes Frank?"

"Cut to the chase. I'm letting you go." An envelope was tossed across the desk to me. "You've done nothing wrong, cutting back. Stuff at home I need to sort..." A hint of frailty fell across his face. "The thing is these sorry bastards need their jobs. I don't know what you're doing 'ere. You can do better than this lad, you and your sodding books, you shouldn't be "'ere." The granite gates behind his eyes closed and my moment with Frank the man was gone, "Go on—piss off."

Much to my surprise Frank never came for his pint of blood. There was no reckoning, no rough justice in a parking lot with me separated from my teeth and spine. I heard no more and have no idea what became of Frank. He could still be there for all I know. This however, I saw for myself— maybe two years later—I was on the London to Glasgow train, sitting opposite a bright-eyed, thin-lipped woman in a bright red coat and silver tipped red leather shoes. Mrs Fogg and yet not Mrs Fogg. We were together for five hours and never said a word to each other. I was an utter stranger to her. I was sorely tempted to lean over and say, "You don't remember me but..."

But I didn't. I wanted to tell her how happy I was to witness her rebirth, but I didn't. I really wanted to, but I didn't. I couldn't, because, of course, she was sitting there, reading her book.

# THE STRAIT ARTIST

The young man in the ill-fitting suit trod spritely through the orange glow of the early morning streetlights. A large battered suitcase hung easy by his side as if he had miles to travel and boundless energy to expend. A lone crow cawed above him in the darkness. The young man stopped, set down his case and turned on his heels to face a still sleeping, crescent cul-de-sac.

His eyes narrowed, inspecting the four moderately sized, dull, colourless, boxy houses before him. Each had its own short drive and a spit of easy to manage, low maintenance garden. Only three of the four drives contained a car. A gleaming 4x4 sat in front of number four, number three had a battered, boxy little thing that clearly hadn't moved for months, whilst number two contained a sporty little shape carefully wrapped in its own fitted sleeping bag. The youth took six steps forward and stared deep into the blackened eyes of the houses and waited for inspiration.

The lone crow hacked its greeting to the morning, and the youth dropped to his knees, and opened his case. Fidgety, delicate fingers ran over the dusty beachhead of chalk and pastel stubs piled carelessly within. One was selected, an indistinct inch of soft round-nosed pastel. He lifted it to his lips, extended a long sharp tongue and licked. Beneath the dust the pastel was coral blue. His sharp angular jaw sliced into an equally angular grin. He pushed his case aside, stretched out on the chill paving slabs and began to draw.

As he worked swirls of dust rose from his fingertips and wafted through the still morning air. When the first bedroom light flickered into life, his suit had already taken on the appearance of a crumpled rainbow—although one seen through a sandstorm. Morning kettles bubbled as the fourth paving stone was completed, transformed into a light filled brook, lined with swishing reeds, alive with silver shinning sticklebacks.

Breakfasts were poured, ignored, toasted and fried and pushed aside as twelve paving stones were completed. Behind the youth, rippled waters danced with dappled light, and the reflection of a swaying willow clung to the surface of the fast-flowing water.

Mrs Simpkins of No. 1, The Crescent, stared at the place she had set and the toast she had buttered and the tea she had made for the emptiness on the other side of the table. A sense of shameful weakness, emptiness and longing rose up in her, as it had done every morning for the last year.

Dave and Jean North of No. 2, decided not to draw the curtains but to spend the day in bed. Dave phoned Jean's work and then Jean phoned Dave's assistant, both trying not to giggle as they expressed their concern for the others health. This done they threw aside the duvet and made passionate, violent but brief love—and then both silently wondered what they'd do with the rest of the day.

In No.3 Caitlin fed her third child at her breast whilst her eight-year-old Joshua, helped Suzy get ready for school. Caitlin had decided she wouldn't be eating breakfast. She'd had to cut the bread down into squares to whittle away the mould that morning, so the kids could eat and now there was none left. She would have to wait until she went shopping which wouldn't be happening until the cheque from her wayward husband cleared and that wasn't going to happen today. She thought about borrowing a loaf from Mrs Simpkins and then she tried to work out how long it had been since she last borrowed from the old lady, and if she'd ever paid her back?

Mr. William Boyce of No.4 tightened his already tight tie until he felt it restrict his Adam's apple. Milly, his wife, busied herself in the kitchen and shushed the children as she urged them to get ready for school without the fuss that so annoyed Daddy. The children quietly chorused their agreement and Mr. Boyce felt a swell of pride in a job well-done. This is how children should be raised, with order and respect for their father's wishes. After all, only one commandment comes with a promise—Honour your Father and Mother and you shall have a long life. Spare the rod and spoil the child may be out of fashion but what the hell does fashion know.

Three minutes later Mr. Boyce was manoeuvring his Brompton through the front door when he saw the dirty, dust covered youth kneeling at the end of his drive. "Excuse me, may I ask what you're doing?" Mr. Boyce demanded as he marched forward. And there it was, right at the end of his drive—a skipping salmon, where no skipping salmon should be.

"Anything wrong darling?" Milly twitched as she came to the door and saw her husband standing silently at the end of the drive and the youth crouched before him. Fearing that her husband had finally lashed out at a deliveryman she ran to his side. And there it was—a jade kingfisher breaking the surface of a fast-flowing stream; "Oh my..."

"Have you ever seen anything like it?" her husband gasped.

"Never...children! Zoe, Samuel, come see this."

Zoe and Samuel Boyce joined their father and looked on in silent awe. "I've never seen anything like it," their father asserted.

"It's very good isn't it Daddy," Sam offered.

"Yes, Zoe it's very good. I say there, you must have been working through the night. It's amazing. What is it for? An arts project, a charity event?"

The dust covered youth lifted his besmirched face and smiled a thin sharp smile and then turned his eyes to Zoe and Samuel and waved. Being good, obedient children who never talked to strangers, they stepped behind their father in fright.

The bedroom curtains at number two opened, quickly followed by the window, "Jean have a look at this, it's incredible."

"What is? Oh wow...who did that, that's amazing, get my camera."

Josh and Suzy emerged from number three and squealed with delight. Suzy ran to the very edge of the sparkling river—Josh was suddenly gripped by the fear that she'd fall in, ran to join her. Together they knelt and peered into see tiny tadpoles peering back at them.

"Mum!" they cried in unison.

"What is it now?" Caitlin snapped as she marched to the door, babe held in place over her shoulder, "Jesus, will you look at that...where did that come from? Suzy come away from the edge."

"It's not real Mum, it's a painting," Suzy shouted over her shoulder.

"Of course, it is," Caitlin reassured herself, "of course it is...but who did it?"

Josh pointed to the dust covered scarecrow crouching over the far end of the river. Cupping his hands to his mouth, for fear that the sound of the river might drown his words, he called out, "Here mister, mister did you do this?"

The chalk encrusted face smiled and nodded and then returned to its work. Josh watched transfixed as the cloud covered man reached across the water and with bold swooping gestures drew the shadow of a swooping dragonfly on the rim of a ripple.

"I wish I could draw, that's bloody brilliant that is."

"Bloody brilliant," Zoe agreed.

Mrs Simpkins, shopping bag in hand, stepped out of number one and immediately jumped back across the threshold. Peeking-out again she began to laugh; "I thought we'd been flooded. Look at that, trout and everything. Isn't that clever. How lovely, but I need to get to the shops. I don't want to ruin it."

Overhearing this, Mr. Boyce judged the distance across the chalk stream, "Good point. Perhaps you should have checked with us first. I need to get to work and I have children who need to get to school, your picture will be ruined."

Taking a piece of pastel in each hand the colour encrusted youth leant out over the path and began working furiously with both hands simultaneously. Dave and Jean joined their neighbours at the edge of the river, spellbound by the manic act of creation happening at their feet.

In three scything strokes, four shinning, life teeming paving stones were obliterated. The watchers gasped in protest at the slaughter. Twisting dust devils spun from the artist's fingers, engulfing him in a cloak of dust, but from the devastation emerged an ancient stone bridge with a family of ducks gliding beneath its reflected arch. They were greeted with a joyful round of applause. The thin youth stood and offered a dusty hand to Mrs Simpkins. Reddening slightly Mrs Simpkins accepted his hand and stepped gently across the ancient bridge. Another round of applause rose from the residents and soon all were gathered on the bridge merrily peering into the watery world below.

"It really is a wonderful piece," Mr. Boyce affirmed as he squared-up to the chalky youth, "will you be doing more?"

"If I may?" the artist replied in a light, thin, dry voice.

"Of course, of course. Nobody minds if this young man does some more work on our street do, they?" Mr. Boyce's bearing demanded his neighbours' compliance.

"Of course not."

"Please do."

"Fantastic! Can you do waterfall?" asked Suzy bouncing on the tip of her toes.

"What about an otter?" wide-eyed Josh asked.

"Can he do swans Daddy?" Samuel enquired.

"Please Daddy, please. Make him do swans Daddy please, please." Zoe chirped excitedly, until her father's firm hand rested on her shoulder.

"Steady now Zoe," Mr. Boyce straightened his back and folded his arms., "what sort of reimbursement are you looking for?"

"I shall leave that to you," the youth demurred gracefully.

"We could all chip in," Mrs Simpkins suggested.

Caitlin felt her throat dry and remembered the tiny slices of toast she'd fed to her children that morning.

"It needn't be money," the artist replied, "a cup of tea would be a good start."

"I can do that," Caitlin jumped in, "soon as I get these two off to school. Go on, you'll see it when you get back tonight."

"Oh Mum."

"Go on. Off with ya."

The youth's bony hand fell across their path, "there will be a waterfall and an otter too," he assured them with his jagged razor smile. Josh and Suzy reluctantly tore themselves away.

Mr. Boyce checked his watch. "Good God. Train to catch, I'm sure they'll look after you." He shook the youth's hand, took his seat on his Brompton and then cycled off at a furious pace—only slightly riled that his hand was smeared with chalk dust.

Once all the protesting children had been sent on their way and the Norths' had taken an albums worth of photos and returned to make their bed—the young artist redoubled his efforts, and settled himself down in front of Mrs Simpkins drive.

Mrs Simpkins returned an hour later with a full shopping bag, she took a moment to tour the scene, laughing at the diving kingfisher, sighing at the fluffiness of the downy ducklings and then she popped across to see Caitlin.

As the door opened, she reached into her bag and produced a loaf of bread and a packet of bacon, "These were on special offer, I thought you could do with them."

"Joan, I haven't..."

Mrs Simpkins waved away the younger woman's awkwardness as if it were a misplaced cobweb, "Do I get a hug of that baby? And what about a cup of tea?"

"Of course," seeing the cloud of dust rising from Joan's drive, Caitlin added, "better make him one too. Said I would. How do you have it love?" she called out.

"Black tea, no sugar. Thank you," was the brisk response.

"I'll pop back," Mrs Simpkins informed Caitlin. She tiptoed along the riverbank until she reached her own drive, which she discovered had become a waterfall, crystal clear and full of sparkling light and a froth-soaked otter.

"Oh my...It's incredible. You're so clever."

The youth flashed her a sharp grin.

"Have you much more to do?"

"Could I do more? I'd like to do more. Would you object Joan?"

"Of course not, you carry on sweetheart. You really are very gifted."

"Then let this be my gift to you Joan."

"Cup of tea. There you go love," said Caitlin as she carried babe and mug to the riverside.

"Let me take that," Mrs Simpkins cooed as she lifted the baby from Caitlin's arms. The youth accepted the tea with a clouded bow and then the two women turned away and headed back inside. Already chatting Mrs Simpkins couldn't help saying, "That was odd. He knew my name?"

"Did he? Maybe Josh told him, you know my boy, talk to anyone..."

The postman came and went, delivering Caitlin's wayward cheque, which brightened her day no end. DHL dropped off boxes for Mr. Boyce and discreetly packaged items for Dave and Jean—tools to extend their blissful nights. And still the youth worked on, wearing out the knees of his trousers, filling the air with dry coloured rain.

Dave and Jean opened their discreet packages in their bedroom but still left the house just before noon. They called across the river to the youth as they unwrapped their sporty little number, "Hay there, we're just going for a drive, sorry if it smudges your work. I'll try not to wheel-spin okay."

Brushing the dust from his elbows the artist sauntered over to the sporty little number and rested a lavender coloured hand on the immaculate windscreen "I really don't think you should do that."

"Why's that then?" Dave enquired jaggedly.

"You'll ruin everybody's day."

"I said I'd be careful."

"We didn't ask you to draw on our street," Jean added for good measure.

"You really shouldn't go," the youth sighed, as he

inspected the grime under his fingernails, "it really will ruin everybody's day."

Dave watched the sassy nobody pick at his grimy fingernails and instantly lost any inclination to be pleasant, "you're not the boss of me pal."

"He's the boss. He owns his own company," Jean taunted.

"That's right I do, and if I want to drive off my own property, in my car, over that doodle, you can't stop me."

"Of course not. But you really shouldn't go."

"Look here you..." Dave felt Jean's hand on his leg.

"Leave it baby, he's not worth it, let's just go. Let him finish his little doodle."

"If you touch my property while I'm away I'll have you," Dave sneered as he started the engine.

The youth stepped back and watched as the car jumped forward, stalled and then restarted. It sped away, erasing a butterfly and muddying the waters with a wheel spin.

Caitlin stepped out to collect her mug when she saw the cloud covered youth inspecting his work, "Joan, I think you should see this."

"What is it dear? Oh my..." Joan stood eyes wide, aghast.

The front of her house had become a photo, or perhaps a picture of a photo she'd long ago misplaced. If not that, then a memory of a perfect scene she'd never had a chance to capture on film. Her face, younger by thirty years, ten feet high, cheek to cheek with a man with the kindest eyes and the warmest smile.

"How did you do that? We lost everything, all our photos in a fire, before we moved here, I didn't have anything to... how did you?"

"It's amazing," Caitlin whispered, "you should take a photo Joan."

"Yes," Mrs Simpkins squeaked and hurried inside.

"That was a very nice thing to do."

"She's a very kind lady."

"Yes, she is, she's been very good to us."

"Would you like something for the children?"

"On the house?"

"Yes. Its only chalk it'll wash off. After all the days fall away so quickly and youth is but a falling leaf."

"I'll make you a sandwich," Caitlin nodded.

Once Mrs Boyce had dropped the kids off at school she'd gone into town and partaken in a little therapeutic shopping. Nothing that would show up on the credit card bill of course—just a cake and a coffee. Followed by a quick rummage through the twelve charity shops that made up the town centre. That done she'd collected her William's suit from the dry cleaners and bumped into that dreadful man who insisted on calling her husband Billy, nobody called him Billy, not even his parents called him Billy, dreadful man. Then it was a quick drive over to the garden centre, they had the best toilets and she could check on the rabbits. Ordinarily she didn't like seeing animals in cages, but the rabbits there always looked happy—is a cage really a cage if you have all you need? Then it was time for lunch, the garden centre's lunches were very reasonable, and she liked it that the girls behind the counter knew not to give her cheese, but always gave her a little extra wholemeal bread. Sometimes, if she got chatting, she could string-out lunch for the best part of an hour, and that only left two hours before the children had to be collected and she had to, had to go home. But there was nobody to talk to today and the lettuce was limp, and her wrist ached from that morning's misunderstanding. She really should try harder, she knew William liked things in a certain way, good God she should know by now. The plate was empty, her coffee cold and all she could bring herself to do was to drive to the school, park outside, turn on Radio 4 and wait, until she had to go home.

Zoe and Samuel piled into the back of the car, keen to get home, and they talked on and on about nothing else but the strange thin man who was painting their world.

"Now children, let's not get too excited now..." Milly heard herself saying and then wondered if it wasn't better for them to get it out of their systems. before their father came home. But yes of course it was, "yes, I'm excited too, I do hope he's...oh I say..." The children squealed like excited puppies as Milly turned the car into their cul-de-sac, and Milly felt tears welling as she fought to catch her breath.

Mrs Simpkins" house had become the most romantic portrait Milly had ever seen, it hurt her heart to look at it. The walls of number two had become the endless expanse of space and ached with the angst of pending eternity. Whilst number three was a thick, verdant jungle crammed with the eyes and tails of hidden animals. But the river, the river was magnificent. Fed by a sparkling waterfall it twisted and flowed and bubbled and glowed with light and life. It was the epitome of river, the perfect river of childhood and storybooks and picnics and endless summer days. As Milly opened the car door, for a split second, she heard the sound of flowing water, she was certain of it, she had to talk herself out of hearing it—it was the sound of her neighbours laughing, wind in the trees, a trick of the mind, nothing more—and once convinced the water stopped flowing.

"Mummy! Mummy look. Isn't it wonderful," Zoe bounced.

"Yes, darling it's wonderful."

"Why isn't our house painted Mummy?" Samuel asked.

"It's not paint its chalk," Zoe huffed.

Samuel swung at his sister—it was a poor punch, more of a shove than a punch really, but she fell hard onto her elbow and immediately burst into tears.

"Samuel! Don't hit your sister. You don't hit girls..." She heard herself say and then saw her own raised hand and thought it was her husbands. "You don't hit people Samuel; you must never hit."

Zoe was up and running. Clutching her elbow, her eyes full of tears and fire, she ran towards the still composing artist.

"Why haven't you done our house?"

"I didn't have permission, and nobody asked."

"Will you please? Please, Mummy please tell him he can," Zoe shouted to her mother who was running to gather her up.

"I'm sorry, I think they're a bit overwhelmed," Milly cringed, "let's wait till Daddy..." this time Milly heard the fear twitching beneath her own words and suddenly she'd heard enough, "no actually, why not. Please go ahead."

"You sure?" the artist asked.

"Absolutely."

A jagged grin split the youth's face, "warped doors often need a shove...or a kick."

William Boyce carried his Brompton from the train, through the ticket gates and checked his watch. He was two minutes ahead of schedule. A pleasant surprise. The bike was reassembled in thirty-two seconds. Not a personal best but not bad for a homeward journey. All in all, it hadn't been a bad day. Yes the start had been a little shaky but that had soon been corrected, and although he hadn't completed everything on today's to-do list, that which hadn't been achieved was not due to his own folly but the incompetence of others—and he did relish pointing that out to his offending, underling, lowlifes; "Not a bad day at all and now, home again, home again jiggity jig."

As Mr. William Boyce turned into The Crescent his Brompton nearly went from under him.

"Good God, what were they thinking?"

A blue arsed baboon, rude and resplendent, pointed at

him from a mighty baobab tree that seemed to be breaking out of number three's bedroom window. Below it, a tiger glared at him, hungry and quivering from behind a lascivious bloom of luscious red flowers. Every leaf, every vine, every vibrant petal shimmered in a steamy, wanton light—it was life untamed, raw and ravenous. What on earth were his neighbours thinking? Number two had been transformed into an outrageous LSD flashback that was clearly designed to corrupt the vulnerable—an outrage, a travesty—he would have it removed at once. Thank God Milly would never be so...

Wide-eyed, open mouthed and reeling William Boyce let the Brompton fall to the road.

He looked to the walls of his castle and at the neighbours gathered before its drawbridge. The sordid gothic horror depicted on it resonated in the accusing eyes of the neighbours who blocked his path.

"Milly, what is this? Get inside at once."

"No, no more,"

"Milly get the children inside at once. I've had a long day and I'm not in the mood for any of your nonsense," he barked in a voice that was cracking under the weight of other's disapproval. Seeing no one move, and Milly shaking in her shoes, he stormed forward. Only to find his way blocked by Mrs. Simpkins" wagging finger.

"Youngman, that's enough."

"Get out of my way..." a suitcase skidded down the path to him. "Get out of my way!"

"Make me," Mrs Simpkins whispered.

Caitlin moved the babe to her other shoulder and pushed the suitcase towards him with her foot, "Time to go now Mr. Boyce."

Boyce turned to see the skinny youth sitting cross-legged amongst a shoal of silver skinned fish. "This was your doing."

"Are you sure of that?"

"Don't make a scene William, please just go," Milly entreated.

Mr. Boyce clenched his fist, bowed his head and fled, one hand holding his case the other leading his Brompton.

Milly laughed and cried, as did her children but then they played in the stream with Josh and Suzy, and laughter seemed to take the lead and be easier to maintain. Soon the children were running from stream to jungle, giggling as they named the pastel animals, birds and insects by their real and adopted names. Tea and sandwiches emerged, cushions and tables were produced, and all was talk and chatter. Until a police car drove into The Crescent, and two officers made their way to number two.

"They're out," Caitlin said.

"Do you know the family?"

"It's just the two of them," Mrs Simpkins added, "is there something wrong."

"We're looking for the Norths."

"Yes, that's them. They left this morning," Mrs Simpkins informed them.

"In their red sports car," Caitlin confirmed.

"A little sporty number," one officer looked to another, "sorry to ruin your day but...would you be able to provide a description."

"What's happened?" Milly asked feeling her stomach turn over.

"Not in front of the children Ma'am. But it's wasn't good..."

"We need to trace their next of kin."

"Sorry to break-up your party, street looks great, who did it?"

A crow cawed and they turned to look for the youth with the ill-fitting suit, but all that remained was a touch of chalk dust drifting in the air.

# THE OXYGEN DEBT
## ON PLANET EARTH NO ONE CAN HEAR YOU SCREAM

"Focus on the sounds around you," the voice on the Relaxation App urges. A smooth voice, the voice of an alpha male. Confident, self-assured but not overbearing.

"Focus on the sounds above you." A very comforting voice. The kind of voice that belongs to a man that wears thick jumpers—and can make them look good.

"Then focus on the sounds to your right." There's a hint of a Scottish lilt to it. So, a jumper wearing, alpha male from somewhere in the Highlands then?

"Let the sounds pass over you." It's not from Edinburgh and definitely not Glaswegian but it's there...East coast for sure. It's been softened by many years south of the border; but it's there still hanging on in there, rolling within the soft vowels.

"Focus on the sounds coming from your left." A fatherly voice, gentle yet persuasive, engaging and attractive but not at all sexual.

"Focus on the sounds that surround you. Let them come and let them go."

But that's the problem. The sounds keep coming,

unpredictable and jarring sounds. Ambulances and arguments. Barking dogs and scratching bugs and the drone of a thousand T. V.'s, doorbells and ringtones and half laughed greetings. Each one rendered impasto against a backdrop of innocuous but ubiquitous household hisses and creaks. The sounds of the tower block aging and stretching, groaning with the weight of the living. The sounds of too many humans in one place. Sounds that never go away. Day after day and then long, long into the night the sound of the living rages on and on.

"Focus on your breathing. Hear the sound of your breathing."

"I'm trying, believe me I'm trying," Brett hissed through clenched teeth and then remembered. "No, no, no. Unclench the teeth. You can't breathe right with clenched teeth. Relax, relax and breathe, breathe."

Not an easy thing to do, breathing. Not anymore. The air was so thick it almost rattled. And when it was in your lungs you could hear the wheeze as it tried to squeeze its way into your red blood cells. The asthma hack; the congested sound of the city, the sound of the suburbs and beyond, beyond, beyond. Cough, cough spew. The national anthem, all the national anthems.; cough, cough, spew.

Suck it in and hold until you can feel it scouring your bronchioles—hold it until your bronchi buck in rebellion and then push, push, push it out and then -

"Breathe in and relax. Stay centred. Let thoughts come and let thoughts go. Be still."

Within the walls the cockroaches rasp, whilst the mice under the floorboards scurry and scratch. Beyond the walls to the right the neighbours cough and laugh. Beyond the walls to the left the neighbours cough and snore. Above and below all snore and hack to the sound of their radio. Across the corridor a baby coughs and cries and coughs again.

Somewhere high above him, came the sound of wrestlers being jeered and coughed at, and then the buildings air conditioning system rattled into life. And so, it was that Brett finally slumped and sighed and snored and coughed and dreamt of crying babies in a wrestling ring with fire breathing dragons and giant Spandex wearing mice.

Brett awoke to silence. A solid silence without clink, chink or crease. A soundless silence.

He was already sweating, hot and aching with a twisting, wringing pain in his chest. He felt as if he was suffocating and so tried to push whatever had climbed onto his face away but there was nothing to push away. Nothing around his neck, nothing over his face but still he was choking; "I'm choking. I must be choking!"

Brett reached down into his throat, pressing three trembling fingers into his oesophagus. His body reacted as it should and sprayed vomit across the room, once, twice and— it was then—as the third spasm kicked in that Brett realised, he couldn't hear himself retching. He couldn't hear the puke splatter or the furniture toppling to the floor as he franticly ran out of the door. He pounded silently on his neighbour's door until his shrivelling lungs began to boil with pain. He needed air. He needed to get outside. Too high up, too many floors to go down; he knew he'd never make it.

Brett fell back into his flat and sprawled across the puke-soaked floor. Frantic as a toppled beetle he crawled to the apartment's caged ledge, that the tower's designers had the gall to call a balcony. The room began to lurch and spin about him. Colours shifted and drained to grey as his fingertips reached the sliding glass doors. Feebly he pushed them aside with the failing strength of desperate need. Adrenaline, panic and the will to live forced his head out into the hot morning air.

Below him the street was filled with the fallen and the

falling. The flailing and the fallen looked up to him, and the grey sky beyond the sky—they gasped with soundless screams. There was no sound, no sound for Brett or anyone else to hear.

Perhaps it was something gleaned from a science class or a documentary that jumped into Brett's head in that last precious moment; a spark of truth withering within hallucinatory asphyxia, an appealing piece of pub quiz trivia retrieved by the dying kindness of consciousness. One of those things that men forlornly retain in order to impress other men or that smashing girl with the shinning eyes—the kind of girl that will never be impressed by such useless trivia. Sound is dependent on air and atmosphere, without atmosphere there is no sound. An impressive fact but, as the unimpressed sneering girl was sure to say; "Duh, without atmosphere there's no life, no nothing stupid." Brett heard her voice in his head or at least he thought he did.

And then there was nothing and no one to hear the silence. The complete silence of Brett and the world passing on, passing on into silence.

# TOE

I've led a privileged and long life but there comes a time, when the back aches and the joints creak so loud they wake you up at night. But it's not just your own failing body telling you it's time to move on. The world has something to say too. Music becomes insufferable noise; people suddenly seem unbearably thick and being around them is just too painful to bear. Aging is a cold, hollow certainty but when you realise that you no longer belong, when you no longer have a useful role to play—that's the time to go. Believe me, I've been there before. And so, in keeping with my own peculiar nature I made my preparations.

Tracking down a chiropodist with an available emergency appointment was a nightmare, hours and hours it took—but eventually I found one in a nearby town who could see me that afternoon. I arrived early, filled out the necessary paperwork, paid the outrageous fee and then waited in the stale, sweaty sock of a waiting room, alongside three sore footed, sour faced patients. An hour after I should have been seen, I was sitting in the vinyl reclining chair, explaining my discomfort. And then came the unveiling—right sock off, "And there it is."

"Oh my..."

"It really is very painful Doctor. It's kept me up for three nights." I always call chiropodists doctor; it makes them more agreeable. I use the magic number three because when linked with troubled sleep, it indicates a level of pain that cannot be ignored and puts the professional in a position where they have to do something.

The chiropodist leaned in close, "I'm sure it is, it looks... well it's very..."

I decided to help him out, "deformed."

"Indeed, I can see there's a problem with the cuticle, perhaps some dietary issues?"

"I doubt it doctor, it's the way my toes go."

"Have you dropped something heavy on it? In the past."

Bless him, he was determined to find some reason for my odd existence. I appreciated the thought but to be honest—I gave up trying years ago—I was busy and wanted to get on. Get on, move on and get out, "No I don't think so, it's just how they go."

"So, it's a family thing? Hereditary."

"Possibly. I don't want to rush you doctor but could you pull it off for me please?"

"Well I think it's going to have to come off yes, but I'm going to have to book you into the local hospital for that..."

"No, I don't think so. Just whip it off. I'd do it myself, but I can't reach. Getting old is a terrible thing."

"I can't do that."

"Yes, you can," I assured him, "I promise I won't tell."

He'd started to sweat and looked genuinely concerned, "But it's really going to hurt."

"I'm sure it won't be as bad as you think, I've had a couple pulled before and it's never been a problem."

The chiropodist watched as I pulled my plump wallet from my pocket, "you've done it before...perhaps we should talk to your GP."

"Go for it Doc, I'm sure I'll be fine. I've only one request. When you're done, let me have the nail."

"It will probably break into pieces."

"Fifty quid extra if it doesn't."

He swallowed hard, looked at the money and got to work. The nail and toe were covered with antiseptic and then the surgical plyers were applied—between you and me there's nothing very surgical about plyers, calling them that just makes the medical type feel more important. Grip tightly, apply pressure to the cuticle, a slight tug to break the skin and then it's a firm jerk up and out—and much to the chiropodist's surprise the nail came out whole with a delicious shrulop. He couldn't hide his relief, "Well that was a lot easier than I thought it would be." He dropped the nail into a metal dish and then began turning it over with the end of his pen, "it really is an odd-looking thing."

I climbed down from the chair and leant over the metal kidney bowl to have a closer look, "yep that's what they look like."

"It looks like a..."

"It does doesn't it," I picked up the nail and held it to the light, "yes, yes it does, doesn't it?"

"Just like..."

"It really does, doesn't it? Well I must be going, thanks awfully."

"It looks like a foetus...I've never seen anything like it. Let me get my camera."

"Actually, I'd rather not if it's all the same with you. But thanks very much, good job, hardly felt a thing. I'll be sure to recommend you to my friends," I shook his hand and made my exit.

I stopped at the butchers on the way home and bought a pound of prime mince and then picked up a litre of full fat milk from the local Co-Op store—shop local, think global.

From that point onward incubation follows a well-ordered process. The nail is placed in a silver dish under the light of a full moon. Pour on fresh milk and three drops of blood—my own, who can afford assistances these days—and a pinch or so of mince. That's it, no great secret, all you can do then is wait for nature to do its thing. You repeat the feeding process nightly, moving slowly on to more substantial meals as you go. Slow and steady, little by little, follow the process and all will be well. And on this occasion the process went very well for the first six months and then that bloody silly Policeman turned up.

"Good morning Sir, I'm sorry to bother you but we've had spate of missing cats in the area."

"Really Officer how awful."

"Six reported in this neighbourhood."

"Really? Six...is that a lot?"

"Yes Sir, more than usual."

"What's usual?"

"Umm...well we expect one of two a month I suppose."

"I see, good to know."

"And the thing is Sir, a man fitting your description has been spotted walking through the streets at night."

"A man fitting my description," I didn't believe that for a moment. I defy description I can assure you of that.

"You Sir, you've been spotted walking through the neighbourhood at night. With a sack. And a fish."

"A fish? I don't think so Officer, a fish. That certainly would be rather suspicious." I have never walked through my neighbourhood with a fish, never, a tin of cat food yes, but never fish.

He clearly didn't appreciate the joke. His voice hardened to a chisel, "Would you mind if I came in and had a look around?"

"No of course not, please come in."

Now you may think me reckless, but this had never happened before and I'm really not much of a liar—well not off the cuff—and so I decided to roll with it. So, in he came, hands behind his back, poking around, being polite and pleasant until we reached the kitchen—and of course, that's when it all went to pot.

"Jesus Christ, what is that?"

"Well I'm not sure what you'd call it really. I suppose an incubus is the old term although it's not really accurate. We've never really found a term we liked..." And that's when I caved in his head with a saucepan.

Yes, it solved a problem, plenty more food to feed the babe but you wouldn't believe the inconvenience it caused. We had to relocate. I used the camper van for a month and then moved us to a static in Skegness...of all places. It was fine, really it was, plump hunting in Skegness. But static caravans are not really designed for our purposes. They never have the cold storage capacity we need. But we got by...kind of...until this morning.

I woke to find my younger, hardly formed self, chewing on my leg. How he'd removed it without waking me I really don't know but he did. I would have wrestled it off him but there really wasn't much point. Such an appetite.

"I arrest you in the name of the law!" it slurped with its mouth full. "I'm taking you in scumbag, you're going down for this." Clearly his recent change of diet had not agreed with him.

"Something you ate dear heart?"

"You're going down! I'm arresting you in the name of..." he then grabbed me by the waist and lunged for my private-parts. Of course, I couldn't let that go, I had to react. Apart from the moral dilemma of one's own incubus going down on oneself, there's the pain to be considered. It just wasn't on—I grabbed the nearest thing to hand, an angle poise lamp and beat his skull into dip.

Seventh months of my life wasted, and now my back is killing me and I've only got one leg. Getting old, it's so undignified. I'm going to have to start all over again. I'm not getting any younger, and now, now I've got to get busy— listen to me go on...here have a little more milk, just a drop more blood then?

# WOOKEY'S WONDERS

"She had a body to die for," the old man wheezed alarmingly. He coughed expelling globules of phlegm across the tight white sheet, tucked like a bib under his chin.

Constable Sims fixed his eyes on his notebook and concentrated on controlling his own rising bile.

"Mr. Wigthorpe, you said you had a crime to report."

The old man turned his head and spat. It landed at the young policeman's feet. "No, I didn't, I said I had a crime to confess. Before it's too late. I want to confess."

"Very well, if you could just tell me..."

"In my own way. If you don't mind. I've waited sixty years to confess, so I'll do it in own time if you don't mind."

Sims tapped the spine of the notebook with his black Bic, "I was going to say, in your own words. If you could tell me in your own words Mr. Wigthorpe that would be fine."

The mucus in the old man's chest gurgled ominously. "Before it's too late ah Officer, before it's too late."

It was 1959 and I was nineteen years old, and there was no better place to be in the world than Soho. As far I was concerned Soho was it. You can keep your New York and your Paris and L.A, who needs them. Soho was the place to be and I wanted to be a writer and that's where the real writers went.

The Coach & Horses, Pillars of Hercules, the Nellie Dean and the Dog & Duck—those were the places were deals were smoothed out, rumours bartered, and the serious drinking done. They'd all spent time in there, Jeffery Barnard, George Melly, Dylan Thomas, all those brilliant mad bastards. Great as they were—and they were—they were just the figure heads, the winners, the poster boys. Muriel's Boys at the Colony Club. But the ship's real crew, the Fleet Street hacks, the unknown poets and the bastard poor scribblers, they were there too—living pen to mouth. I was nineteen and full of dreams. I wanted to be there with them. I wanted to be that most glorious of things, a professional writer.

Soho loved all kinds of fresh meat but fresh meat with money it really loved. That's what I was Officer, fresh meat with a bank balance. I wasn't made of money but my father's death and the settling up of his affairs had left me with a decision. I could either live comfortably for a while or live wildly for a spell or I could try to make my way and risk getting chewed up by Soho's hungry appetite. What to do? Play it safe or take a risk? Life always takes its bites, and the lack of magic in my Dad's life certainly hadn't done him any good. It still chewed him up and far too soon. On my third night "in the smoke" I spotted a chap called Charlie Day, in the Horses. I offered to buy him a pint and some lunch. I don't think Charlie had ever said no to a free drink in his life.

"So, Samuel..."

"Sam please."

"So, Sammy, what's a Young Turk like you doing in this neck of the woods?"

"Apart from drinking with you? I'm looking to become a writer."

"So, where's your typewriter?"

"Back at my flat. I thought I'd better go out and live a little, find something to write about. Maybe get some newspaper work?"

Charlie threw his head back and laughed, "Easy as that is it Sammy, get some newspaper work ah? You're not going to get any assignments sitting in here son. You need to get knocking on some doors."

"I know, but first I've got to know which doors to knock on. And this place is full of doors isn't it Mr. Day...staff reporter for The Express. The man who broke the Scrubbs Sex Scandal."

"Bloody hell, somebody's done their research. I'm impressed."

"Impressed enough to get me an introduction?"

Charlie's head went back again, his laugh crashing off the nicotine yellow ceiling like a falling cymbal, "You know what kid, I do think it is. I do think it is."

And that was it, I started on the paper that week. That was all it took in those days, an introduction, and some balls. Keeping a job was harder of course but being useful and keen helped. The ability to write good copy on time helped even more but you still had to get the chance, a break, something to write, if you wanted to move up to the next level.

I started as the officer runner and general dog's body, but I didn't mind. I soon proved I knew how to check facts and confirm details and even string a line or two together, and that made me useful and that made me popular—especially with old hands like Charlie Day who liked an afternoon drink more than fact checking copy. Also Charlie knew I didn't mind lending a hand, hanging around the late-night clubs with a camera, just in case a face turned up or was thrown out, and he liked it even better that I could run out the few lines he needed written, without interrupting his drinking time.

But what he liked most was getting credit for the scoop, and all it would cost him was a couple of shillings for breakfast. Sooner or later I knew my dedication would come good.

My day came on New Year's Day, the first day of a new decade 1960. I woke that morning to hear Charlie shouting up the stairs of my digs. He was making a terrible row and was waking all my groaning neighbours with his foul mouth.

"Sammy! Where the fuck are you? Sammy! Get up you twat there's work to do. The games in play you bastard, get up!"

I threw on my coat, rushed downstairs just in time to find him trying to navigate his way through a tangle of homemade paperchains. I was feeling suitably rough, but Charlie looked like his New Year hangover could see him through the decade.

"Charlie you look dreadful."

"Can you drive?"

"A bit. I used to drive Dad's delivery truck."

"Good enough." He tossed me a set of keys and staggered out into the road. "Come on Sammy, we need to get back to Streatham."

"You drove here?"

"No, the car followed me. I'm clearly too pissed to drive... anymore."

"Why don't we just take the tube?"

"On a limited service with this head? Are you mad? Drive, come on drive."

"Where's the car?"

"Facing the wrong way down that one-way street over there...somewhere."

Luckily for me and Charlie's head, the traffic was still mercifully sparse. He stretched out in the back of the Austin Princess, pushed his hat down over his eyes and was asleep before we crossed the river.

"Charlie!" I shouted back at him as we approached

Kennington, "Charlie, anywhere in-particular in Streatham?"

"Of course, we're going somewhere in-particular! Silly sod."

"A clue then Charlie, which way you want me to go? Brixton or Clapham?"

"Just stay on this road."

I looked in the mirror. His face was still under his hat, "Which road is that Charlie?"

"Who the hell cares?"

I took us along through Brixton. Charlie's head didn't immerge again until we hit Streatham Green and then he barked, "Take the next left. Left here.... Then the next right and pull over just here."

I pulled up and Charlie hunched forward over the passenger seat and passed me a cigarette. I lit his then mine. Five puffs later he handed me a roll of tenners. I could see it was at least a monkey.

"What's this for?"

"See that house over there with the red door. I want you to go in there and spend that money and then come back here and tell me all about it."

"What do they sell?"

Charlie's hand locked around the back of my neck and squeezed, "Sammy my boy you're about to use your dick in the service of the muse."

"Do what?"

"That there is a house of—as yet unconfirmed—ill repute. You're going to confirm that repute. Tell them Sugar sent you. Tell them it's Sugar's Christmas present to you. Okay?"

"Really? Do I have to?"

"Yes, you do. And Sammy I know it's a bit late like but... Merry Christmas."

I was nineteen, a month off my twentieth birthday and I was in Streatham knocking on a whorehouse door. Does it get any better than that? The door opened a crack, and a sharp female voice hissed; "What do you want?"

"Sugar sent me. It's a gift."

The door opened and an old woman with a crab-apple face, stood in the doorway. I hoped to god she wasn't the whore.

"Come on in sonny, come to see your old Aunty, have you? Lovely boy. How's ya Mum?" she called out to the empty street.

I stepped into the narrow, red carpeted lobby and the door closed sharply behind me. Instantly, Auntie's sweet voice was replaced by a shrill parrot squawk, "Where's the money sonny, we're not here to fuck around." I showed her the roll of notes, "...in that case, you are here to fuck around. How much of that you looking to spend?"

"All of it please."

"Please he says, lovely manners. Well that much is going to buy you a lot of fucking, or some very good fucking. What you want sonny, what wets your whistle?"

My father's warnings about dirty girls and clean girls rang through my head, "Can I have some very good, clean fucking please."

"Bless you, course you can. Cleanest in town." The money was out of my hand and down the front of her dress in a flash. "Wait in there."

She pointed to a pink glossed panel door at the end of the narrow lobby. I tugged at my collar, told my feet to move and walked through into a pink womb of a room. Pink satin drapes covered the walls and windows, an enormous pink bed, littered with pink pillows and cushions, set in the pink pond of a huge fluffy pink fur rug. It was a disturbingly brash take on French boudoir chic. I just stood there looking at the bed. I was completely incapable of getting past the fact that I was looking at such a grotesquely contrived bed, in the back parlour of a house in Streatham, at eleven o'clock in the morning. What would my Father say?

The door opened and in walked the tallest woman I'd ever seen. She was easily 6ft 5 in her bare stocking feet—as we used to say—but her feet were bare, she was bare all the way up to the tip-top of her glorious thighs. She shut the door behind her and then coldly looked me up and down with a sweeping glance. I was taking a lot longer to take her in. I'd never seen anything like her. She was incredible. She had long thick red hair, framing a face that was both cat like and reptilian and yet still completely captivating. She was dressed in a red chiffon negligee that flowed across her broad shoulders as lightly as a puff of smoke—it may have covered her body, but it has hiding nothing. Back in the day, before skinny became the mode, they knew how to build women— that or women knew how to make the most of their build. Look at Marilyn, Bardot, Novak, Loren, god even Doris Day had it going on. But none of them, not even collectively, had the raw sex appeal of the goddess, that stood before me that morning. She was built! She had curves that cars would envy. She had breasts that other breasts yearned to be. She had breasts that you wouldn't dare to call tits, they were grand, they were magnificent. The word heaving was invented for those big bold beauties.

"You can call me Wookey."

"Hello, pleased to meet you Miss Wookey."

"Miss...Maud said you were sweet. What do you want me to call you?"

"Sammy. I mean Sam. My names Samuel but...Sam please."

Her viper cold eyes sparkled, "Oh my, that really is your name isn't it Sweets."

"Yes. Of course."

"You're not really meant to use your real name, didn't

Sugar tell you that?"

"No. I don't think so."

"Well that's just odd. Sugar always tells the punters that, it's his little rule." Her deep brown eyes narrowed as she crossed her arms. under her immaculate bosom.

"So, what's your real name then?" I blurted out and instantly regretted. I was sure I was making a real mess of things.

"Why do you need to know?"

I shrugged and did my best to look nonchalant, but I could feel my face reddening in terror. I was sure to be thrown-out and I'd already parted with Charlie's money. I had no idea if I'd seen enough to prove what he wanted to hear?

"It's a Christmas present from Sugar." I recited idiotically.

"Lucky you...or do you have something on him?"

"No. Just a friend."

"Now I know you're lying. Sugar doesn't do friends." She uncrossed her arms. and sighed, "It doesn't matter. You've paid your money." She tugged at the red ribbon around her neck and the gown slithered to the floor. She was as naked as a smile, "So shall we?"

"Yes please," I spluttered.

"Are you going to take your clothes off, or do you want to keep them on? Do you want me to help?"

"No, no I'll do it," I blurted out. But my brain wasn't listening, and my fingers weren't cooperating, and the buttons on my shirt seemed to have shrunk to miniscule dots.

Wookey stepped across the room in one sweeping stride, grabbed my shirt by its collar, and then with flitting fingers, deftly dealt with my buttons as her beautiful breasts nudged my shoulders.

"Umm look at that...you're going to fit nicely aren't you," she wriggled, "I like men that fit in nice and tight." She dropped my shirt onto the floor and then with a sharp tug, undid my trousers. "There now...let's see...yes. You'll do nicely, I'll do the tightly."

She took hold of my shoulders and shoved me onto the bed. My shoes, socks and trousers were flung to the other side of the room before the bed had even stopped bouncing, and then she was on me.

Her hands gripped my waist and pushed me down hard into the mattress as she raised herself above me. Setting her broad thighs on either side of me she snapped her legs tightly around mine, locking my knees together. Then with a grunt she centred herself above my already prominent centre. Her hips began rocking, undulating above me, delicately brushing the soft heat of herself against me. I need to remind you that I was only nineteen and it was only just 1960. Larkin would have you believe that sex hadn't yet been invented and up to that point my massed experience would certainly have confirmed Mr. Larkin's statement. So, let's just say, nature was taking its course and I was in danger of arriving at the party far too soon. Wookey was clearly a woman from a world apart, and she read the signals perfectly.

"No, you don't," she teased as her hand reached between my legs, grabbed my balls and squeezed. It was like a jet of fire scorching my spine and searing my brain, but it had the desired effect. I was still attentive but not overly so. "Oh Sweets, you are easy money. But nobody leaves before they see my party trick."

She ran her hand up my stomach, across my chest and then pinned my shoulders to the bed, as she shifted her weight above me.

"Now then," she smirked, "let's see." She lowered herself on to me and I felt the moist heat inside her body. I was already to explode again but then she dropped her weight onto my chest, knocking the air out of me. My gasp of surprise amused her, and she giggled in my ear as she rose above me again and gently placed a breast against my lips. Of course, I did what comes naturally. I took it in my mouth and sucked it, I kissed it. I licked her nipple like it was a vanilla ice-cream, and I'd never tasted better, god help me I'd never ever tasted before! Wookey sighed and trilled in appreciation of my efforts, but I was in seventh heaven, I was lapping on Wookey's wonders, lost on the shores of lust...and then slowly ever so slowly she lowered herself down onto me, pressing her breast into my face.

"Yeah, that's it Sweets, take it, take it all in," she panted, pushing down harder.

Her firm nipple pushed against my tongue, her breast filled my mouth, then covered my mouth and then covered my face as she pushed me down into the bed. I couldn't breathe. I couldn't swallow. I was choking on her knockers. I began fighting for air, pushing against her, trying to shift her weight from my chest. But she held me in place like a vice, crushing my chest like a twisting millstone. My mind began to race. I had to get her weight off me. I had to breathe. And then I wasn't thinking anymore, I was reacting, lashing out wildly, my whole-body contorting and writhing under her. I bit her; I sank my teeth in hard, but she just pressed harder. She laughed a sickening, mocking laugh that mixed with the beating pulse in my ears and filled me with despair. I could feel the world drifting away and darkness seeping into me, I was going to die! Then, just on the tip of oblivion, her hips began working, jerking me like a mad piston inside her, and then she threw herself upright and, in that instant, I came, I died, I lived! I was gasping for air, a drowning man raised to life and expelling the life from within him—the thrill of the dichotomy, life and death passing at a hairs breadth. I'd never felt so alive.

I wept, I laughed, I fell in love with Wookey from that moment on. I knew from that one blessed, twisted ejaculation onwards, she was the only one for me.

"All better now?" she smiled as she stroked my thigh.

"Yes. Thank you, Miss."

"Good lad. Go on then...fuck off."

Charlie was asleep in the back of the car when I slumped down in front of the wheel.

"You were quick. How'd it go?"

"Amazing."

"Good lad. Right then, slap up breakfast it is and then you can tell me all about it."

Which of course, god help me, I did. In my defence, I was only nineteen and I'd just been breast-fucked by a goddess. I had to tell someone. I just didn't think to ask myself why Charlie had paid me to go there. I didn't think about the consequences of the things he was asking me. I was still in a joyous fog and I didn't think about anything else until much later that night, when it dawned on me, Charlie was working on a story. I had betrayed Wookey. I regretted it all and would have denied and retracted it all, but by then it was too late.

The story made the front page of The Express the next day, "South London's House of Shame," and the next day all the other papers carried the story of the "Streatham Sex Scandal," the "Seedy Suburbs of Sex." The police raided the house and threw out five girls. Only three were fined. Maud was done for accepting immoral earnings, a small time hood called Simon "Sugar" Johnson was fined for running a bawdyhouse and living off immoral earnings and Wendy "Wookey" Woodcock was charged with affray for knocking off a police officer's helmet.

There was a hundred pound fine and costs to pay, which was a fair bit of money back then. She was more than a little surprised to see who paid the fine for her.

"You?"

"Hello Wookey, I'm so sorry."

"Sorry. You're sorry. So, you fucking should be you little shit. Do you know what you've done to me? Well do you? I've lost everything, all my connections, my contacts, my reputation and the roof over my..."

"You can stay at my place."

"You what? You are fucking unbelievable do you know that? Fucking unbelievable. He turns me over to the papers... and then, and then thinks I'm going to jump into bed with him, just because he paid my bloody fine. Is that your game? Un-fucking bloody believable." She turned her back on me and then those long legs were carrying her off down the road at speed.

"I'm really sorry Wookey I am, I didn't think, I didn't know what I was doing. Charlie's the guy that wrote the story, I work with him." I was almost running to keep up with her. "He gave me the money and told me to go in...and then it was just so amazing, I mean it was so...I just had to tell someone! I didn't think, I couldn't think, I'm sorry!"

She stopped dead and turned so fast I nearly ran into those beautiful breasts, "So what? What difference does that make? I'm still here with nothing."

"I know, but it does mean that I didn't mean to hurt you. I wouldn't hurt you; I think you're incredible. I want to help you."

"Well you've done that now haven't you, now your conscience is clear."

I caught hold of her arm, "No please, I want to help. I meant what I said you can stay at my place. It's not much but it's clean and...and I'd like to have you there."

"I bet you would. Alright, I tell you what, I'll stay but on one condition."

"Whatever you say..."

"No freebees."

She moved in that afternoon. All she had was a suitcase, a

hat box and a vanity case. Arrangements were fairly easy, she just got whatever she wanted. I moved onto the camp-bed and she took my room. She slept late and I went to work and when I got in, she was still in bed. I cooked dinner, which she ate and then returned to her room without a word. That's the way it was for a week, until the first Sunday we spent together.

Sunday was my baking day. My Dad was a baker, a master baker and every Sunday, without fail, despite his long week at work, we would make cakes together. He'd taught me a lot about baking. I'd sit in the shop watching him every morning before school and at weekends. I could make bread, doughnuts, Chelsea buns and lardy cake, in fact I could make just about anything, but Sunday was our cake day, and it was special. I hadn't made a cake since Dad had died but that morning, nothing else would do. It had to be a classic English sponge cake, with buttercream and strawberry jam. Everybody loves a Victoria sponge.

Wookey appeared at the bedroom door, dressed in full-length white satin gown, just as I was sugar dusting the finished cake.

"Smells good Sweets. What's the occasion?"

"It's your first Sunday here. I thought you might like a cake."

Wookey sauntered into the kitchen like a giant iced angel, "You made this for me?"

I nodded and gently slid the cake across the worktop towards her. She fixed her eyes on mine and plunged her index finger through the centre of the cake.

"Feels moist."

"Perhaps I should have waited a bit longer before putting the buttercream in."

"No, I like moist," her eyes shone, and her voice lowered as her finger stirred the cake into a mass of crumbs. "Moist is good. It takes skill to get something that moist...where'd you learn your craft Sweets?"

So, I told her about Dad and his shop and the cancer, and as I talked her eyes softened and the destruction of the cake ceased.

"You really are sweet Sweets." She put two long fingers into her mouth and slowly, deliberately sucked off the buttercream. "Very moist. Cake this good will get you far Sweets. Why aren't you a baker like your Dad?"

"I want to be a writer."

"No money in that Sweets, you've got a skill there, you should use it. Making things that moist is...impressive." The satin gown fell open revealing one milk chocolate coloured nipple. "Cake this good will get you some of the way," she took a fist full of cake and smeared it across her perfectly pert full rounded breasts. "But not all of the way...that okay with you?"

"Sure,"—what else was I going to say?

She grabbed the back of my head and pulled my face down into her cavernous cakey cleavage, locking me there with her strong arms. I licked till my tongue ached. I licked till her breasts glistened and then, when my mouth was full of surgery sweetness, she lifted me off my feet and slammed me against the wall. Her hot firm body squeezed the air out of me as her voluptuous breasts denied me air. My head filled with the scent of her skin and strawberry jam. The world began to spin as I fought against the darkness and then she began to move—jittering, vibrating against me like a manic, ringing alarm clock. I could feel the pressure building inside me as the desperate darkness crushed my lungs and at the point of no return. She threw me to the floor as my body went into spasm. I gasped, I screamed, I came in my pants.

Wookey pushed a chunk of cake into her mouth, lifted the plate above her head and dropped into the floor, "Eat it."

On my hands and knees, I licked the carpet clean with her foot on my back. It was bliss.

When I went to work the next day all I could do was think about her, all I could see was that body. That hair, those glamorous curves, her arm choking the life out of me. Thinking of Wookey filled my day with craving, I longed for the craven pleasures she had shown me. I wanted it again, I wanted more, like the first time, I wanted it all.

"Sammy!" Charlie Day's voice broke into my wanton daydreaming. "Sammy, have you checked the names on that list yet?"

"What list?"

"The list I asked you to check two hours ago. The names of the lost fishermen. Come on Sammy pull your finger out. I need those names before we go to press, come on son. Get a move on."

I finished late that night and when I got home, Wookey was gone. I went crazy. I walked the streets trying to find her. I paid to go into every club I could think of, and asked every goodtime girl I saw, but I couldn't find her anywhere. I went home at four to an empty flat, exhausted but unable to sleep. I was desperate, crushed like a cup cake. She came back at seven that morning.

"Where have you been?"

"Out earning a living."

Her words were so matter of fact and I was so tired that my last reserve of English reserve snapped, "You can't do that! Please you can't do that!" I begged and beseeched, I wailed and ranted abuse and vitriol into her face. Ending with the insubstantial proviso, "...because I love you."

Wookey just smirked, "don't worry about it Sweets it will pass. I've found another place. I'll be out of your hair tomorrow."

"Please don't go...please. I love you. I need you. I'll make you cake."

"Like I said Sweets, cake only gets you so far. I'm going to bed; you need to get to work."

She was right. I was already late. I went into work, but it was a day in hell. A day of self-reproach and crushing guilt. Those mighty pangs of rejection and hate and self-loathing tore me apart. It was like swallowing red hot barbed wire. I couldn't get home quick enough and when I did there was nothing but a piece of paper with an address waiting for me. I wanted to see her, but I knew I couldn't go empty handed. I went to the local shop, spent a fortune and then spent the night baking. I made a sponge cake, a fruit cake, jam tarts, a Blackwell tart and an incredible three-layer chocolate cake and more besides. I booked a taxi first thing the next morning and an hour later, my cakes and I were standing in front of an address in Harrow on the Hill.

"What the fuck are you doing here?" Maud rasped as she opened the door.

"I need to see Wookey."

"Piss off," she spat, slamming the door in my face.

"I won't go until I see Wookey. I'll stand here all day if I have to. I don't think you want me doing that."

I was shown into a newly whitewashed reception area, clearly Wookey had decided to tone down her business premises. Maud took the boxes of cake from me with a sneer and then returned five minutes later.

"Come on then, she'll see you now."

I followed her up the stairs into the front bedroom which still contained stepladders, pots of paint and rolls of wallpaper. In their midst stood Wookey resplendent in white workman's overalls—stretched taut as a drum across that most valiant of busts. The cakes had been cast contemptuously across the bed, my graft and workmanship ruined. My heart sank.

"What do you want Sammy?"

"You…I'm in love with you."

Her laugh was disparaging and mocking, "you're not in love. You're in lust. I know you Sweets, you want Wookey's party trick. You can't get enough of Wookey's wonders."

"No, I want you Wookey I want all of you."

She stepped forward, closing the gap between us to no more than a nipples breadth. I could feel the heat of her, see the fire of intent in her eyes, "So you want a piece of me, do you?"

"I want it all."

"Well you can't have me!" she roared into my face, "but… you can have a piece of me for a price."

"What price?"

"Your cakes are nice, excellent, but they won't do…if you want a piece of me, I want a piece of you."

What could she mean? "I don't understand."

She pulled a long pair of black handled wallpaper scissors from her pocket, "I want a piece of you."

I paled and whimpered but managed to ask, "which piece?"

She took my left hand and held it in front of my face, and closed her long strong fingers over mine, all except the little pinkie finger, "that piece."

"You want," my stomach turned over, "you want my finger?"

"Just a bit," she puckered up her red full lips and blew across my fingers reddening tingling tip. "Just the tip. Not even the first knuckle. Here's the deal. You give to me and I'll give to you, you give of yourself and I'll give you…all I've got."

"Really?"

"Do you need time to think about it?"

I looked at my finger and then at the dull grey blades of the scissors and then at Wookey's heaving barely contained breasts.

"Will you do it for me...please."

Wookey pulled me across the room. Placed my hand onto the stepladder's platform and squeezed my finger tight, "last chance Sweets."

"Do it," I pleaded.

She opened the scissor wide and pinched the tip of my finger between them. "Last, last chance Sweets."

I shut my eyes and looked away, "do it."

CRUNCH—the world became a sea of fire and screaming red pain. And then she caught me up and threw me onto the bed. I screamed as she tore off my clothes. I screamed as she smeared me with cake. I wept as she bit and licked the corrupted confections from me. I wailed as she pushed me into the bed and her breasts into my face. I died, I lived. I came like an electric eel in full flow. Spent and broken, I collapsed into her arms. and slept, bloody and blissfully broken.

I awoke in a bed despoiled by cake, blood, semen and sweat. My hand throbbed but my heart was satisfied.

"Thank you," I mewed sleepily as Wookey cradled me in her arms.

"Don't thank me Sweets, a deals a deal, and our deal stands. You understand that yes?"

"I love you."

"I believe you do Sweets but a girl's got to live...and a deals a deal right."

"Yes Wookey, I understand. A deal is a deal."

"And our deal stands..."

The old man coughed and choked and dispelled another hunk of green goo across the tight white bed sheet.

Sims took his chance, "so Sir, what you're telling me is that some fifty years ago, you participated, willingly in sadomasochistic behaviour, is that it?"

The old man's cough rattled his body like a flagpole in a storm.

"Although it is perverse, if you don't mind me saying. It was done willingly so I can't really see the crime. And it was a long, long time ago, if this Wookey was still on the game there might be some interest, but I don't see the crime."

The old man shook his head furiously, "No, no," again the cough took his breath away. "No...that's the problem Wookey died last year, Wookey is gone."

"So, what's the crime? What crime are you reporting? Who's the criminal here?"

"Me! Damn it! It's me, it's my crime, my fault!"

Sims shut his notebook, "I'm sorry Sir but I just don't think this is anything we can..."

"Wait!" The old man shouted, his chest bubbling like an over boiled pot, "I am the criminal. I loved too well," the old man's teeth sank into the sheet and began tearing and whipping it back and forth, back and forth until, with huge effort he sent it cascading to the floor. "Too well, too long!"

The diapered torso rocked from side to side. Nothing more remained, his arms. and legs had been reduced to seeping suppurating stumps. "I confess! I loved too well too long," he screamed. "Wookey is gone. What is the point of carrying on? I loved too well, too long, I loved too well too long. I loved too well, too long!"

## OTHER TITLES BY NEIL S. REDDY

*Bottle in Avalon: The Good Folk Rule O.K.!*
*iDrip - the Play*
*Interzone Xpress Bookie: A Screenplay*
*Miffed and Peeved in the U.K.*
*The Moor: A Screenplay for a Yorkshire Horror Movie*
*Not Kafka*
*Tales in Liquid Time*
*Taste & See*
*Taxi Sam in Pink Noir*
*Trash Island*

NEIL S. REDDY writer of short stories and strange books lives in Lincolnshire England – but as he's only been there twenty two years he is regarded as a stranger. Son of two London baby-boomers, he was conceived in the summer of love and born in the year of revolution. A confirmed insomniac he has never met a bed he couldn't fall out of. He has an inexplicable aversion to ironing. He left college because they asked him to and then worked for whoever would treat him badly, believing – thanks to George Orwell and Jack London – that's what writers did. His beard is probably older than you and always will be. He thrives on a diet of mushy peas, red wine and cold toast. He is allergic to swimming. He has been known to wear tweed jackets but is most at home in a dressing gown. He takes his tea black – leave the tea-bag in.

OTHER TITLES FROM SINISTER STOAT PRESS

*The Last Book You'll Ever Read* by Scott Hughes
*The Devil Has A Black Dog* by Jonathan W. Thurston
*Spiders in our Bed* by Jonathan W. Thurston
*Body & Blood* edited by Weasel
*Dread: The Sinister Side of Furry Fiction* edited by Weasel
*The Haunted Traveler* edited by Weasel
*Incendiary* edited by Weasel
*Ghostly Pornographers* by Thomas White

CPSIA information can be obtained
at www.ICGtesting.com
Printed in the USA
BVHW031705091120
592889BV00006B/89